WITHDRAWN

Is Dylan getting bored with riding?

"Don't worry so much," Dylan said as they moved out onto the pavement so a horse and rider could go by on the sandy shoulder.

"I'm not," Christina protested.

"Then why are you making such a big deal about cross-country?"

Christina could see Sterling watching her from the trailer. "Because it *is* a big deal. At least it is to me."

"What do you mean by that?"

Christina turned and looked Dylan right in the eyes. "I mean, eventing is important to me."

"It's important to me, too."

"But not important enough to walk the course so you have a better chance of getting Dakota around safely?" Christina asked.

"I can't help it if the play-offs were scheduled for this weekend."

Christina could see the muscles in his jaw tense.

"It's not only that," she said. "You don't ever seem very excited about riding any more."

"Well, I am." Dylan's voice was defensive. "I've just been busy, that's all. Horses aren't my whole life, you know."

"I know." Christina sighed. *That's the problem.*

D0249376

Collect all the books in the
THOROUGHBRED series:

COMING SOON
ASHLEIGH #1:
Lightning's Last Hope

THOROUGHBRED Super Editions:

Ashleigh's Christmas Miracle
Ashleigh's Diary
Ashleigh's Hope
Samantha's Journey

THOROUGHBRED

DYLAN'S CHOICE

CREATED BY
JOANNA CAMPBELL

WRITTEN BY
DALE GASQUE

HarperHorizon
An Imprint of HarperCollinsPublishers

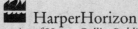

HarperHorizon

An Imprint of HarperCollins*Publishers*

10 East 53rd Street, New York, NY 10022-5299

If you purchased this book without a cover, you should be aware that this book is stolen property. It was reported as "unsold and destroyed" to the publisher and neither the author nor the publisher has received any payment for this "stripped book."

This is a work of fiction. The characters, incidents, and dialogues are products of the author's imagination and are not to be construed as real. Any resemblance to actual events or persons, living or dead, is entirely coincidental.

Copyright © 1998 by Daniel Weiss Associates, Inc., and Joanna Campbell

All rights reserved. No part of this book may be used or reproduced in any manner whatsoever without written permission of the publisher, except in the case of brief quotations embodied in critical articles and reviews. For information address HarperCollins Publishers, 10 East 53rd Street, New York, NY 10022-5299.

HarperCollins books are available at special quantity discounts for bulk purchases for sales promotions, premiums, or fund-raising. For information, please call or write: Special Markets Department, HarperCollins Publishers, 10 East 53rd Street, New York, NY 10022-5299. Telephone: (212) 207-7528. Fax: (212) 207-7222.

ISBN 0-06-106539-0

HarperCollins® and 📚 ® are trademarks of HarperCollins Publishers, Inc. Horizon is a registered trademark used under license from Forbes, Inc.

Cover art © 1998 by Daniel Weiss Associates, Inc.

First printing: September 1998

Printed in the United States of America

Visit HarperHorizon on the World Wide Web at
http://www.harpercollins.com

❖ 10 9 8 7 6 5 4 3 2 1

"OKAY, CHRISTINA. YOU'RE NEXT."

Christina Reese grinned at her riding instructor, Mona Gardener, before gathering her horse's reins. "Let's go, girl," she said to her Thoroughbred mare, Sterling Dream.

Sterling's black-tipped ears flicked back for an instant to catch Christina's words. She raised her finely chiseled head, her muscles quivering in anticipation as though she were still on the racetrack. As soon as Christina closed her legs against the mare's sides, Sterling's whole front end lifted and she went from a stand-still to a canter.

Christina laughed, never tiring of the thrill of riding such a magnificent horse. She let one hand drop to Sterling's dappled gray neck before settling to the task at hand.

"Remember," Mona called from the center of the ring. "I want you to ride this course like the jumps aren't even there. Use the corners to balance her back, and concentrate on keeping her in a slow, even rhythm. Let the jumps just happen."

Think dressage, Christina said to herself as she squeezed with her legs at the same time as she closed her fingers against the movement in the reins. Sterling responded to the half-halt by lifting her back and slowing her pace, staying in the air just a fraction of a second longer for each stride.

"Chin up. Look beyond the fence," Mona's voice reminded her in the background.

Christina glanced at the bright blue and white poles of the three-foot oxer before settling her eyes on the rest of the horses and riders waiting at the far end of the ring.

Three, two, one. Christina silently counted Sterling's hoof beats as the mare carried her to the jump. With a rush of wind, Sterling left the ground and sailed through the air, her nose stretching forward, asking for more rein. Christina's arms followed as she concentrated on staying still in the saddle. They landed with a thump as Sterling, impatient to be off and running, lifted her back in a playful buck.

"Half-halt," Mona shouted, but Christina was already sitting back and quietly checking the mare. She could hear Sterling's tail swishing with disapproval as she grudgingly slowed to a workmanlike canter again.

2

"Good girl," Christina said, turning her shoulders toward the next jump. Sterling's body followed, and five ground-covering strides later, they were over the green coop and approaching the bright yellow and red barrels. Christina could feel Sterling hesitate as they got closer. The mare didn't like the sound the barrels made when she jumped them. The sand pelting back from her hooves as she landed always made her fly forward.

"You can do it," Christina said, her hands firm and her legs keeping a steady pressure against the mare's sides so Sterling wouldn't drift off course. Sterling's strides quickened as if she wanted to get the scary jump over with as fast as possible. Just as Christina was starting her countdown, a robin swooped from a nearby tree, landing on top of one of the ring's fence posts.

That was all the excuse Sterling needed. Christina's left foot came out of the stirrup as Sterling swerved sharply to the side. The five-foot wing of the jump standard loomed in front of them and for one horrible moment, Christina thought Sterling might try to jump it. At the last second, the mare rocked back on her haunches and spun around, shaking Christina loose and sending her flying over the barrels. She had just enough time to see Sterling skim safely past the wing before the ground came up and smacked her in the chin.

Christina spit out a mouthful of sand as she started

to scramble to her feet. She got as far as her hands and knees before she tried to take a breath. Nothing happened.

"Hold still." Mona's voice sounded far away as Christina crawled, struggling to breathe. Just when she thought she'd pass out, her lungs finally cooperated and pulled in great shuddering gulps of air.

It was horrible having the wind knocked out of her like that. She was so grateful to be breathing again that she went along with Mona as the instructor made sure nothing was broken.

"I'm okay now. Really," Christina said, getting to her feet. Her cousin, Melanie Graham, and her best friend, Katie Garrity, clapped as she hobbled over to where Sterling was being held by a tall boy in a navy blue polo shirt and rust-colored breeches. "Thanks, Dylan."

"Don't feel bad about coming off," Dylan Becker said quietly, his brown eyes concerned. "No one could have stayed in the saddle with that big a shy."

Trying to smile, Christina's bottom lip trembled when she looked past Dylan's broad shoulders to his chestnut horse, Dakota, who was nose-to-nose with Sterling. It was normal to be shaky after a fall, even though she didn't feel scared. Surprised or startled maybe, but not scared. Falls like this were part of the territory when you rode hot-blooded Thoroughbreds. Christina sighed. And Sterling had been going along so well, too. But now, as she stroked the mare's sweaty neck, the muscles under the wet, pewter hair were rock-hard with tension.

"I'll give you a leg up," Mona said, coming up behind her as Christina flipped the reins back over Sterling's head. Christina put her left knee into Mona's cupped hands and, on the count of three, sprang into the saddle.

Mona brushed some sand off Christina's navy breeches as she looked up. "You ready to go again?"

Christina laughed, trying to ignore the quivers in her legs and arms. "Only if Sterling will jump it with me this time." She took a deep breath and squeezed Sterling forward.

"Have her trot into it," Mona said. "Your hands and legs should make her feel like she's in a channel and can't duck out."

Christina gritted her teeth as she headed Sterling toward the barrels again. This time the mare was holding back, her head nodding from side to side as she looked for the next horse-eating monster. She trotted up to the base of the jump, hesitating a for second before catapulting herself over with at least a foot to spare. When they landed, Sterling picked up a canter, her hindquarters low to the ground as she scooted away from the scratchy sound of sand pelting metal.

"Keep going," Mona said, waving them on.

Christina nodded, willing Sterling to relax as they turned down the diagonal to the brush jump. In spite of the fact that Christina was sitting back and staying soft with her hands, Sterling surged forward and took off a stride too soon, barely clearing the pine boughs sticking up from the wooden box. Before Christina could try to reorganize, Sterling bolted toward the last fence—a rectangular plywood box painted to look like a stone wall—and flew over it, landing with a teeth-jarring jolt. Christina had to use a lot of leg and hand to bring her back to a walk, and even then, Sterling kept breaking into a nervous jig as they made their way over to the others.

"It was nice up until the barrels," Mona said. "The thing you need to work on is keeping her attention, even when she's scared."

Tell me about it, Christina thought, discouraged that her part of the lesson ended so badly. She watched Katie and her Quarter Horse/Thoroughbred cross, Seabreeze—Bree for short—jump the course without any problems. What Christina found even more annoying was how Melanie was able to keep Christina's outgrown pony, Trib, on course when he tried to run out at the green coop.

"That's the way, Melanie," Mona shouted.

When the lesson was over, Christina couldn't wait to wash off the sand and sweat. Unfortunately she had to ride Sterling back home to Whitebrook Farm without a chance to cool off first.

"By the way," Mona said as they followed her out of the ring, "I was talking to Paige Evans at River Oaks Farm, and she said that there was still room in the

6

novice division of her next event."

"A *recognized* event?" Christina said, suddenly feeling less wilted. Nothing was more exciting than riding the three phases that made up a combined training event—dressage, cross-country, and show jumping.

Mona nodded. "It has a tough cross-country course with lots of hills. If you're still hoping to move up to training level with Sterling later in the fall, this novice course will be good practice."

Perfect, Christina thought. An excited shiver ran down her arms. One thing that she'd discovered at the three-week Saddlebrook Event Camp she'd gone to this summer was that the more challenging the fences, the better Sterling jumped. At least, so far.

"When is it?" Dylan asked. He had just gotten back from the camp, too, and was as gung-ho about eventing as Christina.

"In a few weeks—I'll have to check the exact dates in the Omnibus. Stop by my office and I'll give you some entry forms."

"Are you going to take Dakota?" Christina asked, halting Sterling in the shade of the huge maple in front of the barn. Dylan's big, chestnut Quarter Horse had helped his team come in second at the camp event.

"Yeah, I'd like to," Dylan said, grinning at her as he steered his gelding alongside Sterling. His smile was a little crooked, but Christina thought it was cute.

"Count me out," Melanie said, throwing her right leg over Trib's neck and slipping to the ground like she was going down a slide. "I'm planning to veg-out for the rest of this month." Melanie had gone to Saddlebrook Camp, also, but she wasn't as serious about riding as Christina and Dylan. She preferred hanging out with the young racehorses at Whitebrook, the Thoroughbred breeding and training farm that Christina's parents owned and operated.

"How about you, Katie? You're not going to wimp-out on us, are you?" Christina asked, teasing Melanie with a sidelong look.

Her willowy friend twisted a lock of Seabreeze's black mane around her finger. "I don't know. You guys have a lot more experience than I have." Katie had planned to go to the event camp with them, but at the last minute she had to visit her grandmother instead.

"You rode dressage and cross-country at the Foxwood Acres Horse Trial," Christina pointed out as she dropped her feet from the stirrups and dismounted. "And the only difference between that and a real event is the show jumping phase."

Christina didn't hear Katie's reply because at that moment, a dirt bike burst out of the woods.

Sterling wheeled around, practically lifting Christina off her feet as she threw her head up.

"Whoa," Christina shouted, still hanging onto the reins as the mare lunged backward. Sterling's hind-quarters were almost against the riding-ring fence before Christina was finally able to stop her.

"Easy, girl." Christina put her hand on Sterling's

trembling neck. The mare's dark eyes were huge and her nostrils flared as she watched the dirt-bike rider turn off the engine and take off his red helmet.

"Sorry about that," Chad Walker said, pushing the black hair off his forehead. Sterling snorted at his raised hand. Taking another step backward and jumping, she was startled, when she touched the fence.

"Hi, Chad," Katie said.

"Hey, Katie."

"Just warn me before you start that thing up again," Christina called. Chad was going into eighth grade, as were Melanie, Christina, Dylan, and Katie. He didn't ride, but he was a great athlete. His father ran the summer soccer program and Christina had been on Chad's team the previous summer. She hadn't seen him since June because she decided not to play soccer this year. Training a new horse was keeping her plenty busy.

Why was Chad here anyway? Christina wondered, surprised by how much older he looked than the last time she'd seen him. He used to be shorter than Christina, but now he was shoulder to shoulder with Dylan, though that was where the resemblance ended. Chad's build reminded her of a Quarter Horse—muscular and solid—whereas Dylan was long and streamlined like a Thoroughbred.

"Still hanging out with the girls, huh, Becker?" Chad said, rocking the bike back to push the kickstand down. "When are you going to get back to a real sport?"

Christina rolled her eyes. Chad was always giving Dylan a hard time about riding.

But Dylan just laughed. "When you tell me where you stole *that* piece of junk."

"What are you calling junk? This is *real* horse-power." Chad swung his leg over the seat and stood beside the bike, patting its silver handlebars. "Dad and I just finished rebuilding it. He got it cheap from a guy who'd wiped out one too many times."

"Here," Dylan said, holding Dakota's reins out to Chad. "I want to check it out."

When Chad took the reins, Christina noticed he kept his arm straight and tense, trying to stay as far away from Dakota's hooves as possible.

Dylan swung his leg over the long, black seat and pretended to rev the engine. "How do I look?" he asked, ducking close to the handlebars and leering.

Chad snorted. "Pretty wimpy in those tight pants."

Dylan looked down like he'd forgotten he was wearing riding breeches and boots. He laughed, too, but Christina could see the tips of his ears were red.

"Hey," Chad said. "Did you hear about the soccer team my dad pulled together? We're going to be in the county's all-star games."

"Oh yeah?" Dylan said, looking up with interest.

"Yeah. We've been practicing for a few weeks. Too bad you were away. We could have used you on defense."

"Man," Dylan said, shaking his head in disappointment. "When's the first game?"

"Two weeks. They start on a Monday, and the final playoffs are on the weekend. Dad's trying to get the cable company to tape them." While Chad was talking, Dakota inched his way closer to him, his pinkish-brown nose sniffing the back of Chad's neck.

"Hey." Chad jumped like he'd been bitten. Dakota rocked back and shook his head, blowing out through his nose. "Gross. I've got horse snot all over me," Chad said, looking a little green and running his arm across his face to wipe off the wetness.

"You'll live, Walker," Dylan said, slapping Chad on the back before taking Dakota's reins and heading to the barn, chuckling.

"Stop by my house later and you can take the bike for a spin," Chad shouted after him.

Dylan looked back. "I'll be there."

"You going to be done soon?" Chad said, shoving his hands into his back pockets and grinning at Katie.

Katie's dimples flashed. "In about ten minutes. I have to untack Bree and sponge her off."

What was this? Christina wondered. *Were Katie and Chad a couple now?* Christina looked from one to the other. She hadn't been in touch with Katie since before camp started. She'd tried calling her a couple of times in the three days since she'd been back from camp, but when no one answered, she had assumed Katie was still at her grandmother's.

Katie noticed her staring. "I'll tell you later," she mouthed.

11

"Who was that guy?" Melanie asked as she and Christina were riding their horses home after the lesson. During the school year, Melanie lived with her father, Christina's Uncle Will, in New York City. Melanie's mother had died when Melanie was only three and her father worked in the music industry and traveled a lot. After Melanie had gotten into some trouble earlier in the summer, her father had sent her to Kentucky to live with Christina's family, thinking it would do her good to be away from home for a while.

"I'm sorry," Christina said, hitting herself in the head. "I forgot to introduce you. That was Chad Walker from school."

"He's cute," Melanie commented.

"I guess—if you like jocks." Christina personally preferred guys like Dylan who weren't always strutting around and showing off. "His father coaches everything and Chad's always first-string."

"Because of his father?"

Christina shook her head. "No, because he's good. As good as Dylan."

Melanie waved her riding bat at the deerflies buzzing around Trib's ears as they rode down the shady trail. "So, how long has Katie been going with him?"

"I don't know. It must have started while we were at camp. I'm going to call her later and find out." Christina slapped a fly on Sterling's neck. When she looked at her hand, it was covered with blood. "Ugh," she said, squeezing Sterling into a trot. "Let's get out of here before we're eaten alive."

Christina forgot about Katie and Chad when she and Melanie trotted though the woods. As her seat automatically rose and fell to the rhythm of Sterling's steps, she felt the waistband of her breeches to make sure the entry form Mona had given her was still tucked in.

She could hardly wait until the River Oaks Event. It was going to be great, especially since Dylan and Katie were competing, too. They could start their training together right away and even the work would be a blast. Having friends who liked to do the same things was the best. Christina couldn't remember ever having a more perfect summer.

2

"WHAT'S THIS I HEAR ABOUT YOU FALLING OFF?"

Christina peeked under Sterling's neck and grinned at her mother. With her dark hair drawn back into a ponytail and the collar of her polo shirt standing up on one side, Ashleigh Griffen looked more like an exercise girl than the Kentucky Derby winning jockey that she was.

"News travels fast," Christina said, making a cloud of dust as she pulled the rubber curry comb across the soft body brush she'd been using to make Sterling's pewter coat gleam.

"Especially around here," Ashleigh teased. At Whitebrook Farm, horses were the center of everything. "I ran into Mona at the post office."

That explained it. Mona was her mother's best friend. "It was no big deal," Christina said, giving

15

Sterling a pat before stretching an arm over the stall door to let herself out.

"Good thing," her mother said. "One broken bone a year is enough, thank you!"

Christina agreed. When she'd fallen off Sterling earlier in the summer and fractured her wrist, it had almost kept her from going to the Foxwood Acres Horse Trial. Fortunately Cassidy Smith, a top-notch rider from Mona's barn, kept Sterling in training until Christina could ride again. Christina couldn't wait to show Cassidy how much Sterling had learned at the camp, but Cassidy had taken her two horses away on the New England show circuit for a month and wouldn't be back until school started.

"Did Mona tell you about the River Oaks Event?" Christina asked as she tossed the brushes into her grooming kit. Sterling stuck her head over the heavy oak door and nibbled Christina's hair. "Cut that out," Christina said, snatching her strawberry-blond braid out of Sterling's mouth. She dug into her pocket and offered the last bit of carrot instead.

"She did." Her mother raised one eyebrow as she added, "It sounds like you need to put a lot of miles on Sterling so she can get used to the world off the race-track. You don't want her shying along the River Oaks cross-country course when she should be paying attention."

"I know," Christina said, the memory of her fall still fresh in her head. "I'll be glad when she doesn't think that everything that moves is out to get her."

"And speaking of mileage . . ." Ashleigh said, putting her arm around Christina as they headed down the neatly swept aisle, ". . . don't forget Missy. She was a pistol while you were away at camp."

Christina smiled, picturing Missy, the seven-month-old Thoroughbred weanling she was in charge of training, rocketing around her stall like the racehorse she would become some day. It would be more than a year before she would be ridden, but until then, Christina would groom, lead, and handle her so her manners would be in place before she got too big to control.

"I wish someone had spent more time getting Sterling used to noises and distractions when she was little," Christina said. "Then she might not be so easily spooked."

"Don't forget she's been off the track for less than three months," her mother said, grabbing a halter and lead shank off the row of hooks outside the tack-room door. "Take her on a lot of trail rides and road hacks and she'll get better." Ashleigh paused outside the door of a broodmare that had arrived the day before for breeding. "And have fun with her, honey. Training doesn't have to be all work."

Christina considered what her mom had said. Lately Sterling had had more ring work than just fun hacks through fields and trails. Maybe she should call Katie and Dylan to see if they wanted to go for a long ride with her tomorrow morning.

"Hey, Christina."

Christina turned and grinned as a red-headed boy her age led a leggy, black foal toward her. Kevin, the son of Whitebrook's head trainer, Ian McLean, had also been assigned a weanling to handle.

"How's Rascal doing?" Christina reached out to stroke the place around the foal's muzzle where the fuzzy baby-fur had started to shed, leaving behind hair that was as smooth and dark as a seal's. Even though Kevin lived right on the farm in the cottage on the far side of the barns and was almost like a brother, Christina hadn't seen much of him since she'd come back from camp three days ago.

"He's a beaut," Kevin said, his green eyes lighting up. "Stood real well when the blacksmith trimmed his hooves last week."

"How did Missy do?" Christina asked, wincing as she anticipated his answer. Missy wasn't crazy about having her hind feet picked up.

"She got away once. But after she figured out she could stand on three legs without falling over, she wasn't too bad." He pulled an envelope with a red, white, and blue border out of his back pocket. "I got a letter from Samantha if you want to read it."

Samantha was Kevin's older half-sister. They had the same father, but different mothers. When Samantha was twelve, her mother was killed in a riding accident, and Samantha was in college by the time Ian married Beth and Kevin was born. Christina knew that Kevin missed Samantha since she had moved to Ireland six years ago. Even though Samantha was so much older than Kevin, they had a special relationship and wrote each other often.

"Sure. I'll read it later," Christina said, grabbing the letter away from Rascal's inquiring nose just in the nick of time. "If you wait a second, I'll get Melanie and we can work the weanlings together." Her cousin wouldn't have to be asked twice. Melanie loved handling Terry, the dainty bay weanling she had been assigned.

Kevin glanced at his watch. "Can't. Mom's taking me into town for new cleats. I busted out of mine at soccer practice this morning."

"Are you on the all-star team, too?" Christina asked. "Chad was telling us about it."

"Yeah. Jacob's playing, too, " Kevin said, grinning. "Too bad Dylan was away at camp during tryouts. We could have used him."

Kevin, Dylan, and Jacob had played together on the same baseball team earlier in the summer. Christina had gone to a lot of the games to watch Dylan pitch.

"I think Dylan wishes he was playing, too." Christina pushed Rascal's nose away from her pocket. "He's going to be pretty busy getting ready for the River Oaks Event, though. Katie and I are going, too." Christina had a brainstorm. "You want to take Jasper on a hack with me, and maybe Dylan and Katie tomorrow

19

morning? If you go, Melanie might come," Christina added as she noticed him hesitating. It was no secret that Melanie and Kevin liked each other.

Kevin looked tempted, but he shook his head. "I've got soccer practice."

"Kevin!" Beth McLean shaded her eyes as she stood in front of the barn, peering inside.

"Gotta run," Kevin said, waving to his mother before opening Rascal's stall door.

Christina pulled her sweaty T-shirt away from her body as she headed to the house to change into something cooler. Poor Kevin. She was glad she didn't have anything cutting into her time with Sterling.

By the time Christina and Sterling emerged from the woods by Gardener Farm the next morning, the sun was already hot.

"Hi," Christina called to Matt Dawson, Mona's head groom. He was helping unload a truck that was backed up close to the rear of the barn. Christina could smell the sweet, dry hay from twenty feet away.

"Hi, Chris. Dylan's out front." Matt picked up a bale with one arm and tossed it in the hayloft.

"Thanks," Christina said, automatically sliding her leg behind the girth to keep Sterling straight. The mare was trying to swing her hindquarters to one side so she could keep an eye on the truck as they walked by. "Silly girl. It won't bite."

Dylan was just mounting Dakota when Christina rounded the corner. His face lit up when he saw her. "Hey, Chris."

Christina's stomach gave a little hop. "Morning," she said, feeling the warmth from his smile.

"Are you up for the ten-mile loop?"

"Sure." Christina peered into the barn. She couldn't see very far down the aisle because of the bright sunlight. "Where's Katie?"

"She called the barn while I was tacking up," Dylan said, putting his left leg in front of the saddle and lifting the leather flap so he could tighten the girth another notch. Dakota swished his tail in annoyance. "She said she couldn't come after all."

That's funny, Christina thought. *Katie sounded excited about going on a long hack when they'd talked on the phone last night.* Of course, she'd sounded even more enthusiastic when she gave Christina a blow-by-blow account of how she and Chad had started hanging out at the town pool when she'd gotten back from her grandmother's.

"I guess it's just the two of us, then," Christina said. "Melanie decided to stay at Whitebrook and ride Pirate today." Even though Melanie liked riding Trib at lessons and on trail rides, Pirate was her real horse. She had saved his life after he lost his sight and had to stop racing. The high-spirited, young Thoroughbred had stopped eating at first, he was so depressed. Melanie figured out that he still needed to be a part of the busy racing world, so she trained him to be a track pony—a horse that accompanies young racers around the track.

"Okay by me," Dylan said, gathering his reins. "Let's go."

They rode side by side, Dakota's steady Quarter Horse attitude rubbing off on Sterling. Christina could tell the horses were happy to be going out. Their ears, pricked eagerly forward, shone like silver and copper in the sunlight.

"I'm glad you wanted to go on a hack," Dylan said, one hand holding the reins and the other resting on the top of his thigh. "I missed just being able to ride without having to think all the time about *getting dat horse in de proper frame.*"

Christina giggled. He sounded just like Frieda Bruder, the strict German riding instructor at Camp Saddlebrook. "And all those sitting trots," she added. "Remember when Melanie asked Perky if she could ride with the gel pad on *top* of the saddle?"

The metal stirrups clinked as their legs bumped together. Christina started to move Sterling away, but Dylan reached out and took her hand, his eyes on her face. When she smiled, he shifted so their fingers were laced together, and gave them a squeeze.

"Camp was fun, but I'm glad to be getting back to normal again," Dylan continued, as if it were the most natural thing in the world to be riding along the edge of a field holding hands.

"I know what you mean," Christina said, hoping

he couldn't feel her pulse racing. She liked his warm, strong grip. "Sometimes I wished I could just hop on Sterling and get away from everyone for a while."

Dylan nodded. "Me too."

"Really?" Christina was surprised. He and Sean, the only other boy at Camp Saddlebrook, had seemed to enjoy being the center of attention.

"Yeah. There wasn't anyone I could really talk to the way I do with you. You know, about the future. I mean, you were there, but there were always so many other kids around."

Christina smiled. "I know what you mean." She and Dylan were aiming for the top. They both talked about riding in the Four-Star events some day—maybe even the Olympics. And they were going to make it, too, because they had what it took: determination and a true love of horses.

When they turned onto the trail, Dylan dropped her hand. "Ladies first," he said with a gallant sweep of his arm.

"You just don't want me tailgating you," Christina retorted, laughing. In true racehorse fashion, Sterling pulled a lot when she had to follow behind another horse, and usually ended up dangerously close to the horse in front of her. Dylan was nice about always dropping back on narrow trails. "You ready to trot?" Christina called back over her shoulder.

"Sure," Dylan said. "When we get to the galloping field, I want to work on my half-seat."

"Me too." The half-seat position was used for jumping and galloping. It was a balance between sitting in the saddle and standing in the stirrups, taking the rider's seat off the horse's back to make it easier for the animal to jump. Christina had to work hard to keep her seat as close to the saddle as possible without actually touching it. If she stood too high in the stirrups and Sterling shied, she could fall off.

They didn't talk as they trotted along. Christina let her hips follow Sterling's stride as they enjoyed the cool, damp feel of the woods. Sterling was startled when a chipmunk scrambled across a rotten log, but her hoof-beats were muffled in the pine needles, thick and spongy on the path. As Christina admired the rays of sun that found their way through the telephone-pole sized pine trees, a sticky thread brushed against her cheek.

"Ugh. Spider webs," she said, wiping her face.

"Why do you think I let you go first?"

"Oh, you—" Christina stuck her tongue out at him.

By the time the trail opened into the field, the horses were warmed up and pulling at their bits. Christina turned to the left and Dylan came up beside her.

"Maybe if we go clockwise, Sterling won't think it's a race," Dylan said, waving away the gnats that had appeared with the sun.

Christina shrugged. "It's worth a try."

Sterling leaped forward into a trot a fraction of a

second before Christina even closed her legs on the mare's sides. It was as though their brains were wired together, she thought as she posted to Sterling's ground-covering strides.

The field was about as wide as a soccer field and three times as long. Christina loved the way it was surrounded by trees and brush, except for the couple of places that trails broke through. Even the trails were hard to see, though. Sometimes Christina accidentally rode past them and had to backtrack.

The field had been hayed recently, and new shoots of green were just starting to show in the golden stubble. If any groundhogs moved in since the last time they checked the field, their holes would be easy to spot.

"Ready?" Dylan asked. He was already in a half-seat position, his heels firmly down as his knees acted like springs, absorbing the bounce of the trot.

Christina nodded, admiring the way Dylan rode like he was a part of Dakota. As soon as Christina's seat left the saddle, Sterling's neck and shoulders rose and the mare leaped forward.

"Steady," Christina said, her fingers moving up the reins so she would have a better feel of Sterling's mouth. The mare settled into an even, long-reaching gallop that left Dakota, with his shorter, Quarter Horse strides, behind. The air whistled past Christina's helmet as Sterling began to blow, her breath rhythmically puffing with each stride. Sterling's pace quickened as she pulled at Christina's hands, asking for more rein.

"No," Christina said, closing her legs and fingers as she sat back in the saddle, trying to rebalance Sterling and bring her head up. Sterling was leaning too far forward, galloping as though she were on a smooth track instead of uneven ground where a stumble could send her toppling. Christina needed to shift more of the mare's weight back to her hind legs before they'd get a rounder, event-horse gallop.

She glanced over her shoulder to make sure Dylan was out of the way before turning Sterling toward the middle of the field. It would be easier to collect and reorganize her when they were riding a circle. Sterling's ears went back, listening as Christina's voice went, "Whoa, whoa, whoa," in the rhythm of her stride as they spiraled inward. The mare shook her head and added some playful bucks before she rocked back and settled into the balanced stride Christina wanted.

"That's the way," Christina said, letting her right rein slacken as she stroked Sterling's neck. They were cantering in a dressage-sized circle. As Dakota turned the corner at the end of the field and galloped past, Christina could feel Sterling's muscles tense in protest.

"It's too hard running next to another horse, isn't it," she said. So instead of following Dakota, Christina turned off the circle and headed Sterling back in the direction they'd come.

"Good girl." The wind snatched Christina's words

as Sterling listened to her half-halts and continued a rounded canter down the field. There was nothing like the feeling of the power building beneath the saddle as Sterling's ears flicked back and forth, waiting to be released.

"Okay," Christina said, finally relenting and allowing Sterling to lengthen. She concentrated on keeping her seat close to the saddle with her heels down, toes pointed slightly out to lock her legs into place. Dylan was already at the far end of the field, watching. Christina pretended she and Sterling had jumped the last fence at the Rolex—one of the most important three-day event competitions—and were galloping to the finish.

A flash of color caught her eye a split second before Sterling swerved sharply to the left, jerking her off-balance and snapping her neck back like she was the last skater in a crack-the-whip game. Sterling scooted, almost cantering sideways across the field. Before Christina could get all the way back in the saddle, the mare stopped dead in her tracks, spinning around to face her attacker. It happened so fast that Christina ended up lying on Sterling's neck, struggling to keep from slipping off.

"Whoa," Christina said, determined to push herself back over the pommel and into the saddle before Sterling moved and shook her fragile hold. She had lost her stirrups and reins and the only thing that was keeping her from sliding off Sterling's narrow neck was a fistful of mane—and luck.

Sterling, rooted to the ground in fear, cooperated as Christina wiggled back into the saddle, shoved her feet into the stirrups, and quickly took up the reins. The mare's heart was hammering under Christina's legs as she shifted the helmet back from her eyes and saw what had caused the problem. Two people were perched on a dirt bike at the edge of the trail Christina and Dylan had ridden into the field minutes before.

"Are you okay?" Katie asked as she climbed off the back of Chad's dirt bike and hurried across the field toward Christina.

Sterling lifted her head even higher, snorting through her nose.

"It wasn't even running," Chad called. His hands were in the air, palms up.

Christina wiped the sweat out of her eyes. "It would have been better if it had," she yelled back. "Then Sterling would have known you were there."

"Poor girl," Katie said, slowing as she came alongside. She reached up to pat Sterling's neck. "I'm sorry we scared you like that."

"I thought you were a goner," Dylan said as he rode up. Dakota was keeping a watchful eye on the dirt bike.

"Me too," Christina said. She was glad Sterling had given her a chance to slide back into the saddle. Falling off two days in a row would have been too much.

"Katie, I have to get to practice," Chad called.

Dylan glanced at Sterling. "Better wait until we move before you start that thing up."

"I thought you were going to ride with us," Christina said, looking down at Katie.

Her friend blushed. "I decided to go later. I wanted to watch Chad play soccer." She gave Christina an apologetic shrug before jogging back to the dirt bike. "Call you tonight," she said as she climbed on, circling her arms around Chad's waist.

"Okay." Christina shortened her reins and pressed her calves against Sterling's sides. "Come on, girl. We'd better get out of here."

Except for Sterling almost dumping her, the ride was perfect. After trotting and cantering for miles, she and Dylan loosened the reins so they were just holding the buckle, and let the horses walk the rest of the way home. They rode along, their feet dangling out of the stirrups as they talked. "If we keep this up, I bet both these guys will be ready to event training level by the time school starts." Christina stretched way forward to scratch under Sterling's ear.

Dylan made a face. "Don't remind me about school," he said.

"Why? You always make honors."

"It's not that." Dylan sighed. "I just don't get to ride as much."

"You should get the bus to drop you off at Mona's," Christina said. "Then you'd have plenty of time."

"Yeah, but then Chad and Jacob give me grief."

"What do they care?"

Dylan shrugged. "Don't you get bugged to hang out? You know, at the arcade or something?"

Christina never thought about it. She went to sleepovers and basketball games with her friends on weekends, but going home to ride after school was as much a routine as eating dinner or brushing her teeth. "I guess everyone knows I have stuff to do around the farm."

"Yeah, well you're lucky. If I go to the barn every day, the guys make it seem like I have a problem."

"That's stupid."

Dylan reached for her hand. "Yeah, I guess you're right. I won't mind as much as long as I can keep riding like this, with you."

Dylan rode with her back to Whitebrook. He got off to get a quick drink from the hose before returning to Gardener Farm. "I'll check Mona's Omnibus when I get back to see what events we could go to this fall," he said, handing Christina the hose.

She took a drink and wiped her mouth with the back of her hand. "Great."

"Missed a drop," Dylan said, touching her cheek with his finger. Just as Christina was wondering if he was going to kiss her, Sterling shoved her forward, rubbing her nose along Christina's back. Dylan steadied her with his hands.

"Sorry," Christina said, giggling.

Dylan leaned down and kissed her quickly on the

lips. "I'm not. Sterling's helping me out."

Christina couldn't stop grinning as she untacked Sterling after Dylan left. She was lucky to have a boyfriend who was a good friend, too. And best of all, Dylan loved horses as much as she did.

"Chris! Telephone." Her father's voice drifted through the bathroom door later that day just as Christina finished drying off. She slipped an oversized United States Combined Training Association T-shirt over a pair of boxer shorts and sprinted into her bedroom.

"What's going on?" she asked, glad that Katie remembered to call.

"Uh, hi," a deep voice answered. "This is Dylan."

Dylan! Christina pushed her dirty riding breeches onto the floor and flopped on the bed. "Sorry. I thought you were Katie."

"Guess what?"

"What?" She twisted her finger in the cord, waiting.

"Chad Walker's father called me because he's looking for another goalie. Matt Jarvis broke his leg."

"Playing soccer?"

"Skateboarding."

"That's too bad." Christina had seen Matt around town jumping curbs with his board. He was really good.

"Anyway, Mr. Walker wants me to be on the all-star team."

31

Christina could hear the excitement in Dylan's voice. "Wow. Are you going to do it?"

"Sure," Dylan said as if she had said something crazy. "Why not?"

Why not? Christina echoed to herself. And why was her stomach sinking? "I guess I just wondered if you could do it when you haven't been to any of their practices." What she really wondered was whether he would still have time to ride with her.

"Mr. Walker said he and Chad would work extra with me. I'm good on defense, but I guess I could use more time in the goal."

"You can do it," Christina said, feeling bad for being selfish. "You're so good at sports."

"Thanks," Dylan said. "Anyway, there's almost two weeks until our first game, so I can catch up."

Christina looked at the horse calendar hanging beside the bed. The River Oaks Event was two weeks and two days away. "You're still going to take Dakota to the event, aren't you?"

"Sure. The games start the Monday before."

"That's good," Christina said, flopping back down and pushing her feet against the wall. "For a second, there, I thought you were going to poop out on me."

Dylan cleared his throat. "There's only one thing."

"What?"

"We have practice every day at nine o'clock."

"But that's the best time to ride," Christina moaned, thinking about how much fun it had been to ride the loop with Dylan that morning.

"I know," Dylan said. He sounded disappointed, too.

Christina ran her tongue over her front teeth. "I guess we could ride in the afternoon."

"Yeah. Or if it's really hot, maybe we can go after dinner when it's cooler."

"Okay. Do you want to ride here after lunch tomorrow?" Christina asked. "We can go on the cross-country trail Kevin and I made—even if the jumps are a little dinky."

"Sure," Dylan said. "Just a second."

Christina heard mumbling in the background. In a minute, Dylan was back.

"I've got to get off so Dad can use the phone. See you around one o'clock tomorrow."

"All right. And congratulations for getting on the all-star team."

"Thanks."

After she hung up, Christina just lay there on her bed listening to the crickets outside. Even though she was trying to feel happy for Dylan that he got to play on the all-star team after all, she couldn't brush off the uneasy feeling in her stomach.

Stop it, she told herself. Dylan was too serious a rider to let soccer interfere with his horse. There was plenty of time to do both.

Wasn't there?

AT TWELVE-THIRTY THE NEXT DAY, STERLING WAS STANDING in the aisle on cross-ties while Christina worked on her mane.

"Hold still," she scolded as Sterling fidgeted forward out of reach. Christina grabbed the mare's halter—almost losing her balance and falling off the step stool in the process—and pulled her back into place.

"You're such a big baby," she continued, taking smaller locks of hair to shorten with the special blade she held in her hand. "It's not as if I'm pulling it out at the roots."

Sterling stamped her foot, then lowered her head to scratch her knee with her teeth. Christina was used to this evasive tactic. She leaned against Sterling's pointed withers at the base of her neck and turned to face the square fan mounted from the ceiling. Even in a tank top and cotton breeches she was sweaty.

An engine noise caught her ear and she ducked to see out the barn door. Chad was riding up the driveway on his dirt bike. *What was he doing here?*

Sterling's ears pricked forward in interest. She didn't mind moving vehicles coming up the driveway. It was when they burst out of trails that they bothered her.

Christina climbed off the stool and dragged it out of reach of Sterling's hooves before she went to see what Chad wanted. The sun made her squint as she left the shady barn aisle. When the biker pulled off his helmet, she stopped in her tracks.

"Dylan? I thought you were Chad." Christina grinned as she walked over to the bike. "What are you doing here?"

"What do you mean, Chad?" Dylan teased. "I thought we were the ones with a riding date."

Christina blushed at the word *date*. "Sooooo, where's Dakota?" she said, turning away and resting her hand on the second helmet strapped to the back of the seat. "And what are you doing with Chad's dirt bike?"

"He let me take it home after practice because he had an orthodontist appointment." Dylan lifted his eyebrows. "Want to take a ride?"

"On that?"

"Sure. It can really fly."

Christina looked to see if her parents were around to object. "Okay," she said. "Let me stick Sterling back into her stall. I'll just be a sec."

The motorcycle helmet was a lot heavier than her riding one. Bigger, too. As soon as she swung her leg over the bike, she and Dylan accidentally bumped heads. "Sorry," she giggled.

"Hang on." Dylan stood, straddling the bike as he kicked down on the starter. Christina grabbed the underside of the seat as the bike tipped a little to one side, but there wasn't much to hold on to. When the engine roared to a start, Dylan called over his shoulder, "Put your arms around my waist."

It felt funny holding onto him. They had slow danced together at camp, but this was different; more personal somehow. "Okay," she said, laughing when they bumped helmets again. She could smell the laundry detergent in his shirt. It was nice.

Dylan rode carefully down the driveway, almost slowing to a stop before veering off between the double fence dividing the two front fields. When he leaned to the right, tipping the bike, Christina automatically threw her weight to the left.

"Lean with me or it messes up my balance," Dylan called back. "Don't worry. I won't let us tip over."

Christina started to lean left again when Dylan turned right after the field, but quickly corrected herself. She was surprised at how neatly the bike carved the turn.

"Isn't this cool?" Dylan asked, his voice bouncing up and down as they rode the trail. "Wait until we get to the field and I can open it up."

Christina tried to look where they were going, but every time she leaned around Dylan's shoulder, the bike tilted. She watched the trees go by on either side of her instead. It was weird being down so low. She was used to looking at the woods from Sterling's back.

"Hang on," Dylan shouted as they flew out of the woods into a field. "Yeeeeeee-haaaaa."

Christina's head snapped as the bike shot forward. She tightened her grip around Dylan's waist and wondered whether it would hurt as much to fall off a dirt bike as it did to hit the ground from a horse.

"Slow down," Christina finally yelled, as her stomach bounced up to her throat.

Dylan cut the throttle and they rolled to a stop. "Don't you like it?"

Christina threw her leg over the seat and got off. "I can't see enough to tell." One thing she knew was that if she was going to go that fast again, she wanted to be the one driving. "How do you work this thing, anyway?"

Dylan showed her how the throttle in the right grip turned toward her to give it gas.

Bbudddddring-ing-ing-ing-ing. The engine sounded like an overgrown chain saw with a cold, Christina thought, letting go of the handle. "Is that the brake?" She pointed to the silver lever that looked like a heavy-duty version of a bicycle hand-brake.

"No, that's the clutch," Dylan explained. "When it's time to shift gears, I have to let the clutch out slowly and give it gas, or else the engine will stall."

"How do you shift the gears?" she said, looking around the gas tank for a stick with a knob or something.

"With your foot." Dylan pushed a silver pedal with his left toe until it clicked. "All the way down is first gear. That's the one you start on. Then, when you pick up speed, you hook your toe under the pedal and click it up once like this," he demonstrated. "Now you're in second."

"What do you do for third gear?"

"Just keep clicking up one. It's simple."

"Can I try?" Christina said, running her hand along the handlebars.

Dylan thought for a moment, then shrugged. "I guess so. But don't crash it, or Chad will kill me." He flashed his crooked smile.

It took a while to get the hang of letting the clutch out at the same time as she turned the throttle. Sometimes she did it too fast and the bike lurched forward or stalled. Other times she gave it too much gas and it sounded as if she were on a gigantic motorcycle. But after she circled the field using all five gears without too much lurching and bucking, she rode back to Dylan.

"Hop on," she said.

The bike was definitely more fun when she was the one in charge. The wind rushing in her face and the ground flying past reminded her of galloping as they raced around the field, darting in and out of trails.

"Slow down," Dylan said, pretending to be scared.

"Never," Christina called back, the rushing air

snatching her words. She liked the feeling of power as she opened the throttle further and zoomed down the field. No wonder Chad and Dylan thought dirt bikes were fun.

"I don't know how much gas we have," Dylan shouted over the roar of the engine.

"Okay," Christina said, cutting the engine. The silence was welcome as they coasted to a stop.

After Dylan showed her how to put the kickstand down, they walked over to the edge of the field and flopped down in the shade.

"How was your first practice?" Christina asked, reaching for a piece of red clover.

"Good," Dylan said. "When we scrimmaged, only one ball got by me into the net."

"Who else is on the team?"

Dylan ran down the names of the guys, most of whom Christina knew. She tried to listen when he talked about their strengths or weaknesses, but her thoughts started drifting away. Finally she laid back in the grass with her arms behind her head, watching the clouds.

"Castle," she said when Dylan finished.

Dylan stretched out beside her. "It's a dragon," he argued. "See its tail?"

It was peaceful watching the wind rearrange the white puffs. Christina imagined an invisible hand parting the clouds like they were bubbles in a giant, blue bathtub. "Now it looks like a dog."

"Or a dirt bike." Dylan hitched himself up so he was

40

leaning back on his elbows. "I wouldn't mind having a dirt bike until I get my license. With so many trails around, I could get almost anywhere I wanted without having to go on the road."

Christina pulled herself up on one elbow. "I always wanted to have a four-wheeler for the farm, but Dad says they're too expensive."

"Chad thinks I could pick up a used bike for around seven hundred dollars."

"Oh, well. Seven hundred dollars. That's nothing," she joked.

"I almost have that much in the bank," Dylan said. "You know, birthday and Christmas money from my grandparents."

"But I thought you were saving for a dressage saddle." Christina wiggled to a sitting position.

Dylan sat up, too, pulling a blade of grass out of a clump and smoothing it over his thumb. "I don't know," he said, shrugging. "My all-purpose saddle is okay."

Christina's saddle was an all-purpose, too, which meant it was shaped for both dressage and jumping. She had used Mona's dressage saddle once, though, and had to admit it was easier to ride with a deep seat and long legs. And since Dylan was pretty serious about dressage, it hadn't surprised her when he told her at camp that he was saving for a dressage saddle.

But she was surprised now. And a little bothered, too, even though she was trying not to be. After all, it *was* his money.

41

Dylan blew into the grass blade, making it whistle. The high-pitched squawk cut into the peaceful quiet. She glanced around, half-expecting to see Sterling's ears pricking forward to listen. But Sterling was back in her stall, waiting.

"We'd better go," Christina said, jumping to her feet. "I want to get riding."

"Okay with you if I drive this time?" Dylan said, playfully draping his arm across her shoulders as they walked to the bike.

"Sure," Christina said. "Just keep it under sixty."

They took the shorter way back, but even then, Christina was eager to get off.

"How long will it take you to get Dakota?" she asked as she pulled the sweaty helmet off and began fastening it to the seat.

Dylan shoved his hands in his jeans pockets and slowly let out his breath. "Actually, I promised I'd take this back to Chad by three. Then he's going to help me with my goal kicks."

"Well, shoot," Christina said. She had been looking forward to riding with just Dylan again. "You should have told me you didn't have time to do both."

Dylan's face fell. "I thought you'd like trying the bike out."

"I did." Christina tried to explain. "But I didn't know it would mean we couldn't work the horses together. I was hoping you'd help me with dressage."

"I could help you tomorrow afternoon."

Christina smiled as she brushed the curly hairs away from her forehead. "That would be great."

"Hey, you want to watch soccer practice tomorrow?" Dylan asked as he got back on the bike.

Christina kicked a pebble while she thought about it. They weren't going to ride until after lunch tomorrow, and she could always work Missy before supper. "Yeah, sure."

"Great." Dylan rocked the bike off its stand and started the engine. "See you then."

Christina watched until he disappeared into the trail. As she turned to walk into the barn, something was bothering her, but she couldn't quite put a finger on what. It wasn't until Sterling nickered to her over the stall door that the niggling thought came to her. Dylan hadn't mentioned Dakota once all afternoon.

"No way would *I* ever choose a dirt bike over you," Christina said as she rode Sterling out of the ring an hour later. Her mare's black-tipped ears flicked to catch her words before returning to their usual, alert position.

Christina leaned back, patting Sterling's rump as they followed the tractor road to the cross-country trail she and Kevin had made. The jumps weren't much— just fallen trees and branches they'd dragged across the path—but they were still fun to canter over. And she'd promised Sterling a run since they'd worked so hard on dressage.

"Your muscles are getting better up here, I think," Christina said, one hand on the reins while the other tried to judge the size of the muscles on either side of Sterling's backbone. "By the time we go to the event, I bet your topline will be filled out."

For eventing, Sterling needed to develop different muscles from the ones she'd used for racing. The tucked-up-belly look of a racing fit horse was gone now, and her ribs were filling out as she put on weight. But developing a topline—the muscles along the top of the back and neck that helped her carry Christina without losing her natural balance—took a lot more time.

Just like learning about dressage took time, Christina thought as they passed some yearlings gathered under a tree. Christina used to think that dressage was nothing more than riding around a little ring in front of a judge. Nothing very exciting unless you were in a higher level and did fancy movements such as passage and piaffe.

Now Christina understood that dressage was more than riding circles and making transitions in the right place. It was teaching Sterling to move as freely and easily with Christina on her back as she did when she was riderless in the field. Christina loved to watch Sterling when she was turned out with the other horses. Her tail would lift, and her legs seemed suspended in air for seconds between each step. She was born knowing how to do flying changes and pirouettes. Dressage was helping Christina and Sterling learn how to move together, so they would be better partners when they jumped.

Sterling lifted her head and quickened her walk as they approached the opening to the trail.

Christina laughed. "Okay, girl. You've been patient enough." She locked her calves into Sterling's sides, gathering the reins in one fell swoop as Sterling eagerly leaped into a canter. The mare's nose stretched forward as she looked for the first fence.

It was a big pine tree whose upturned roots and porcupine branches kept it suspended a foot off the ground. Kevin had trimmed the top of the trunk so nothing would scrape the horses' bellies. As they approached the fence, Christina shifted her weight back and closed her fingers on the reins to check Sterling's speed. Even though the jump was only two feet tall, she didn't want Sterling to blast over it with one big canter stride.

Sterling tossed her head, ignoring Christina's signals and jumped the log just the way Mona didn't like, with her back hollow and her back legs trailing.

"Sterling," Christina complained. "I'm going to make you trot the rest of the jumps if you can't do better than that." She sat in the saddle and closed her legs and hands in a firm, half-halt, grinning when Sterling responded by shifting her weight back and lifting her front end. It was a neat feeling—sort of like when the bow of a powerboat goes up as it increases its speed.

"O-kay!" Christina said, going back into her half-seat position. "Let's eat them up."

Sterling was totally underneath her as they wound through the woods, the mare listening to Christina's

45

commands and easily handling flying lead changes at every bend. Christina felt like she could point her in any direction and the mare would follow without hesitation. They were a team.

The last bend in the trail before it opened into the field was a ninety-degree turn. Sterling hesitated, expecting Christina to pull her back to a trot as usual. But Christina sat in the saddle, her right leg on the girth and her left leg behind the girth, squeezing to help Sterling bend correctly into the turn.

"Good girl," Christina said, stretching forward to quickly run her hand alongside Sterling's silver streaked mane. It was a little uneven at the top.

Suddenly Sterling startled. Christina's head jerked up and blood pulsated in her ears. Directly in front of them, where the trail should have been opening to a field, stretched a newly fallen pine, its boughs reaching upward like prickly, green hands.

It was big, too big to jump with the forklike branches ready to rake Sterling's legs or belly. Christina sat, her legs glued to Sterling's sides as she tried to halt her. But Sterling rocked back, almost rearing in the air as she gathered her body into a giant spring.

4

SHE'S GOING TO JUMP. SHE THINKS I WANT HER TO JUMP IT.
As the thoughts raced through Christina's head, Sterling took one more stride and left the ground. Christina's hands automatically stretched toward Sterling's ears, and her heels pushed down as far as they could go. A flutter of mane touched her cheek as she held her breath, waiting to hit ground again.

They kept going up in the tunnel of green. Then Sterling's head began to drop as the pine needles moved past like the brushes in a car wash. Christina could feel Sterling twist underneath the saddle, and a split-second later, the mare's feet hit the ground and they were cantering into sunshine so bright it made Christina squint. This time when Christina asked Sterling to stop, the mare listened.

"Wow," she said, wishing her heart didn't feel like

it was going to jump out of her chest. "I can't believe we made it."

Sterling was blowing hard, too. Christina got off and did a quick inspection, but the mare's legs and stomach were completely unscratched. Christina patted Sterling with relief before leading her back to the tree for a closer look. The trunk of the tree was about three feet off the ground, but as they got closer, Christina realized that some of the branches were higher than her head. Even if Sterling had managed to slip between the limbs, she still must have jumped almost five feet.

Sterling pushed against her back, knocking her forward. Christina grinned as she turned around and offered her palms to rub against instead.

"If you can jump like that," she said as she took a step back to brace herself against Sterling's enthusiastic nose, "we are really going to go places, you and I."

With impeccable timing, Sterling nodded her head and snorted, sending white flecks of foam everywhere.

"It was incredible," Christina told Melanie later that afternoon. "I mean, she could have stopped in time, but she didn't. She *wanted* to jump that tree. She's a natural." Christina winced as she peeled the backs of her legs off the beanbag chair and wiggled onto the bedroom carpet. It was too hot for vinyl.

Melanie's mouth hung open as she brushed polish

on her toenails. Three bottles were lined up on the old-fashioned windowsill that was a foot off the floor of Christina's bedroom. So far, Melanie's toes were red and blue on her right foot, red and yellow on her left.

"Do you think the yellow looks sick?" she asked, running her hand through her short, almost white-blond hair as she tilted her head. "Maybe I should paint blue over it and see if it turns green."

"I can tell you're really impressed with our jump," Christina said.

"I was impressed for the first ten minutes you talked about it," Melanie answered, waving her legs back and forth like a pair of scissors. "Now I'm thinking you'd better get a life."

Christina was in too good a mood to be insulted. "I have a life, and it's horses. What could be better than that?"

"Boys, clothes, food, music, sleep." Melanie put up a finger for each word. "Should I keep going?"

"I like that stuff, too." Christina pulled a *Practical Horseman* out of the basket by her beanbag chair and flipped it open. "But with eventing, I can't go halfway. It's like training for a triathalon; we've got to work every day or Sterling won't be ready." Christina sighed.

"What?" Melanie said, pulling herself into a sitting position.

"Well, Katie canceled out on riding with us because she wanted to be with Chad. And all Dylan talked about today was soccer and the dirt bike."

Melanie pretended to look solemn. "What could they be thinking of? Next thing you know, they'll be robbing banks."

"I'm serious," Christina said, throwing the magazine at her cousin.

"I know you're serious. That's the problem. You're serious enough for all three of you." Melanie tossed the magazine over her head. "If you don't give Sterling a day off sometimes, both of you will go bonkers."

"I *am*. She's getting one day off a week."

"Tomorrow's Saturday. Give her a rest and come with me to the all-star practice. I promised Kevin I'd watch."

"Okay," Christina said, laughing when Melanie's jaw dropped. Her cousin didn't know that Christina had already told Dylan she'd come.

"But only because Sterling's legs might need a rest after that *spectacular* jump," Christina continued, grinning wickedly. "Did I tell you about it?"

"Hopeless. You're really hopeless," Melanie said, covering her ears.

It was a perfect Saturday morning, Christina thought as she pedaled beside Melanie on her mountain bike. Sunny but cool enough so the air blowing past raised goose bumps on her arms as they made their way to the recreation field to watch Kevin and Dylan practice.

"Look," Melanie said, taking both hands off the handlebars for a second before grabbing them again with a screech when the front wheel wobbled. She had been practicing in the driveway, but still wasn't too good at it yet.

"You're getting there." Christina let go of the grips and crossed her arms over her chest as she pedaled. "Try sitting up straighter."

By the time they got to the recreation field, Melanie could ride without hands for five seconds. "There's Katie," she said as they left the asphalt and bounced across the playground.

Katie waved. "Chris, Mel. Over here."

Dylan turned to look. His smile made Christina's stomach flutter all the way across the field.

Christina was used to going to Dylan and Kevin's baseball games in the spring. It seemed weird, though, to be sitting on the sidelines of the soccer field instead of playing. Up until this year, Christina had been in the town's intramural soccer program with most of the boys on the team. It was pretty laid back, with practice and scrimmages on Tuesday evenings and games on Saturday mornings. This was the first year the town had even pulled together a team to be in the All-Star County League.

"So, why aren't there any girls on the team?" Christina asked.

Katie plucked at the grass. "I think they have a separate league."

"I'm surprised you didn't try out." Katie was fast with a ball.

"Nobody wanted to organize a girls' team," Katie said. "Mr. Walker is coaching because of Chad. He's already talking about trying to get him into college on a soccer scholarship, and that's five years away."

Christina shrugged. "No harm in planning ahead." She had already figured out what she wanted to be doing in five years. Sterling would be nine, the perfect age for going to the Olympics.

At first there wasn't a lot to watch—just dribbling and kicking drills. But when Chad's father divided the team for a scrimmage, Christina wished she were playing, too.

The boys had gotten a lot stronger in the last year, though. Kevin could slip past most of them with his ball-handling skills, and Jacob Mowery, who had played shortstop on their Bluejays baseball team, was fast. Christina felt a little sorry for Matt Jarvis, who was sitting behind the goal with his cast propped up in a chair as he gave Dylan advice from time to time. Dylan was amazing, though, as he dove for the ball, then kicked it clear to the other half of the playing field. He and Chad were the obvious stars, but Christina wouldn't want to be on the same field with Chad when he challenged the ball. Mr. Walker had to talk to him a couple of times for being too aggressive.

"So what do you think?" Dylan said, dropping down in the grass beside her when the coach called a water break. His face was sweaty and red.

"It's a good team," Christina said. "I don't see how you can make yourself dive for the ball when you're in goal. Doesn't it hurt?"

Chad clapped Dylan on the shoulder. "We're tough. Stuff like that doesn't bother us the way it does girls." He was hamming it up for Katie, but Christina knew he was partly serious.

"Give me a break," Christina said, laughing at Chad. "Girls are plenty tough. When's the last time you fell off a galloping horse?"

"Ha. Piece of cake," Chad said.

"Yeah, I bet you've never even been on a horse." Melanie threw a clump of grass at him.

"Sure I have. Ten at once, to be exact."

Kevin, Dylan, and Katie laughed before Christina caught on. "We're not talking about horsepower," she said. "Anyone can learn to ride a dirt bike. Right, Katie?"

Katie shrugged. "I haven't tried yet."

"Katie likes riding with me," Chad said with a wink.

Christina felt like throwing up. What was with this macho act? She was about to say something about riding double when Dylan opened his eyes wide, shaking his head a little.

He doesn't know Dylan taught me how to drive the dirt bike, Christina realized. She tried hard to keep a straight face as she played along. "How long does it take to learn how to ride a dirt bike?"

Dylan looked relieved.

"About ten minutes," Chad answered.

"Can you learn how to ride a horse in ten minutes, Chad?" Melanie said.

Kevin laughed. "I think they're ganging up on you."

"I'll let you try Bree if you'll teach me how to ride your dirt bike," Katie said.

Christina jumped in. "If you learned to ride, we could all go out on trail rides together."

Katie leaned into Chad. "It would be fun."

"Come on, guys," Chad said, looking cornered. "Help me out here."

"You can borrow a pair of my breeches," Dylan offered with a grin.

Chad blanched. "Look, I'll get on a horse. But the tight pants are out."

"It's a start," Kevin said, raising an eyebrow at Dylan.

By the end of practice, they had it all planned out. They would meet at Mona's on Sunday and give Chad a riding lesson on Seabreeze. Then they could all ride bareback to the river for a picnic.

"Who are you going to stick me with?" Chad said. "A black stallion?"

"You can ride double with me on Bree," Katie said. "Chris and I have done it a lot."

Chad grinned. "I think I can handle that."

"Let's all ride double," Kevin suggested.

Melanie looked pleased with the prospect. "We'd better take Jasper, though. I don't think I could stay on Trib bareback if he got cranky."

"You want to ride Dakota with me?" Dylan said. "I bet Sterling's backbone is on the sharp side."

"Sounds good." Christina would rather ride double with Dylan on a horse than a dirt bike any day.

Melanie dug her elbow into Christina's side when Mr. Walker called the boys back to practice. "Let's bake cookies to bring with us."

"You and Kevin, Christina and Dylan, and me and Chad," Katie said, her eyes sparkling. "It's perfect."

Christina grinned. She'd been feeling a little guilty having a boyfriend to ride with when Katie didn't. Maybe Chad would turn out to like horses, after all.

Christina led Seabreeze out of the barn on Sunday as Katie ran to the tack room to get a helmet. Melanie and Kevin were sitting on the fence, their backs to the ring as they let Jasper and Dakota snooze in the shade. Chad was trying to figure out how to put on a pair of the leather chaps and Dylan was bent over double, laughing.

"So why am I the only one around here that has to dress up like a cowboy?" Chad said, when Dylan stopped laughing long enough to help him.

"Shorts are okay for bareback riding, but you'll get

pinched on the inside of your legs by the stirrup leathers if you have bare skin," Dylan explained.

When the chaps were finally on, Chad strutted around with his thumbs tucked into the buckle part. "These beat the heck out of those tights you wear, Becker."

Christina rolled her eyes as she brought Bree up beside him. The riding breeches jokes were getting a little old.

"So, where's the ladder?" Chad said. "I'm going to need some rungs if you want me to climb up on that thing."

"Seabreeze does not appreciate being called a thing, do you, girl?" Christina said, turning to stroke Bree's velvety black nose. "Don't worry. We'll let you use the mounting block."

Chad followed her over to the big, square platform. "This for skateboards or something?" he quipped as he walked up the ramp.

Dylan laughed. "No, it's for ski jumps, you idiot."

Sometimes Dylan was as bad as Chad. "Actually, it's for wheelchairs," Christina explained. "Mona has a riding program for handicapped kids."

"Cute," Katie said, admiring the chaps. "See if this fits." She handed up the larger of the two helmets she'd grabbed from Mona's extras.

"Oh, man," Chad whined. "I have to wear this?" Katie helped him adjust the strap as Christina positioned Bree.

"Now put your right foot in the stirrup," Melanie called.

"You'd like that, wouldn't you?" Chad said with a grin.

Christina smiled. She had seen beginners mount by putting their right foot into the stirrup instead of their left. One kid had actually followed through and ended up backwards on the horse.

Even with the mounting block, Chad had a little trouble lifting his leg. "These chaps are too tight," he complained. "I can hardly bend my knee." With Dylan's help, he finally managed to get in the saddle. Dylan helped him get his feet into the stirrups the right way, with the ball of his foot resting on the bottom of the stirrup iron. Katie showed him how to hold the reins. "Now keep your thumbs pointing up," she told him before clucking Bree into a walk. Christina stifled a laugh when he took her directions too literally and held his thumbs away from his fists as though he had two plums stuck on them.

"Here, like this," Christina said, jogging up beside Chad. She fixed his hands the right way.

"Thanks." Chad shook his head. "I feel pretty dumb up here."

"You'll get used to it. Everyone feels that way at first." Or so she'd heard. Christina couldn't even remember learning to ride. Her parents used to sit her in front of their saddles before she could walk—she'd grown up riding.

Chad looked so awkward on Bree, Christina almost felt sorry for him. And with everyone barking out directions like heels down, head up, hands down, eyes up, he just got stiffer and stiffer.

"You're trying too hard," Christina finally said. "Just relax and pretend you're on your dirt bike."

Bree's ears flicked back when Chad went, "Vroom, vroom."

"Sorry." He reached forward with one rein to pat her neck. Chad did better after that pat, like he'd figured out he could move without falling off.

"Do you want to try a trot?" Katie asked after about ten minutes of practice. Chad was walking, halting, and turning on his own now, though Katie was walking by Bree's shoulder, just in case.

Chad was game, and Christina was surprised to see that, after a little bit of bouncing, he figured out the up-down motion of posting pretty fast. He really was a good athlete.

"Not bad," Dylan said. "How about a canter?"

"No thanks. I think I'll quit while I'm ahead."

While Katie took off Seabreeze's saddle, Dylan and Christina went over to take Dakota from Melanie.

"Want to drive?" Dylan joked, holding out the reins.

Christina grabbed one of the backpacks that was leaning up against the tree. "That's okay. I'll ride in back with the food."

"Yeah," Melanie said, shouldering the other backpack. "We don't trust you guys with the chocolate chip cookies." She glared at Kevin.

Kevin looked longingly at the pack. "I only ate two."

Melanie fed Seabreeze handfuls of grass while Kevin and Dylan helped Chad get up behind Katie. "Whoa," he said, grabbing onto Katie as she nudged Bree into a walk. "It's slippery without a saddle. We're not going to trot, are we?"

"I'll think about it," Katie said. Christina could tell she liked being in charge.

Dylan took a handful of mane, and swung up on Dakota from the ground.

Chad laughed. "Show-off."

"Want a hand?" Dylan asked.

Christina nodded, reaching up with her left hand to grab Dylan's arm just below the elbow. He held her arm in the same place to make a link.

Christina stood beside Dylan's foot, facing Dakota's tail. She took a deep breath and said, "On the count of three. One, two—" The last number was a grunt as she swung her right leg as hard as she could. Even with Dylan pulling, the added weight of the backpack made it harder to jump into the air high enough so she could twist and land facing forward. Her leg brushed Dakota's hindquarters, but she made it.

"Nice job," Dylan said, squeezing her hand before he let it go.

Melanie looked at them with her mouth open. "So, when did you learn to do that?"

"We'll never tell," Dylan said in a mysterious voice.

Christina poked him in the back before answering. "Gymkhana races. It's easy when you start with ponies."

"Want to try?" Kevin said, holding out his arm.

Melanie had to tilt her head to look at Jasper's back. "I think I'll stick with the mounting block, thank you."

"Wait a minute," Melanie asked after she scrambled up behind Kevin. "Since we can't take a mounting block with us, does this mean I have to eat lunch on Jasper? No offense," she added, reaching behind to pat the Anglo-Arab's tawny hindquarters.

Chad didn't look very happy at the prospect, either, but everyone else laughed.

"We can use the rocks by the Tarzan swing to climb back on," Kevin said.

"Tarzan swing?" Chad echoed, his eyes lighting up. "Now you're talking. Let's go!"

5

"YOU OKAY?" DYLAN SAID, TURNING HIS HEAD UNTIL Christina could smell the faint, peppermint scent of his toothpaste.

"Perfect." The sun was warm on her bare legs, but Dakota's back was a little slippery under her shorts. When she tightened her arms around Dylan's waist, he squeezed them for a second with his elbows before letting his hands follow Dakota's bobbing head. It felt great riding along the edge of Mona's hay field, the long grass tickling her calves as she and Dylan swayed together to Dakota's stride. She pulled a long stalk of timothy grass out of its sheath and used the fuzzy end to tickle Dylan's skin. He rubbed his neck twice before he figured out what she was doing.

"Hey, you," he said, grabbing the stalk from her and putting the sweet, green end in his mouth.

"Hillbilly," Christina teased, glancing behind to see how the others were doing.

Chad reached out to grab a piece of hay, too, almost losing his balance.

"Watch it," Katie said, giggling. "You just about pulled me off."

"Maybe we should go back and get my Yamaha."

"Bree's not fast enough for you? Hang on."

Fortunately for Chad, Bree's part-Quarter Horse breeding came through and her slow jog didn't bounce her riders up any more than the mechanical-horse ride in front of the five-and-dime store in town.

"Cool," Chad said with a surprised look on his face.

Soon they were all trotting, with Melanie screaming once when she slid too far back on Jasper and he kicked his hind end up in protest.

"He doesn't like it if you bounce on his kidneys," Kevin said. "That's why I told you to scoot up closer."

"You should have said that in the first place," Melanie said, rolling her eyes. "I thought you were just flirting."

"Uh, oh. The sodas." Christina could hear the clink of aluminum in her back pack. "We'd better walk the rest of the way if we don't want the cans to explode."

The breeze off the river felt good against her wet legs when Christina slid off Dakota's sweaty back. Kevin and Dylan rigged up a picket line between two trees so the horses could be tied up during lunch.

"Cook-ies," Kevin said, when he left the three horses happily grazing in the shade in their halters. He lunged for Melanie's backpack.

Melanie twisted away and ran up the rocks. "Say please."

"Please." Kevin ran after her, but Melanie dodged and went around a tree.

"Say 'Pretty please with sugar on top.'"

"Pretty please with—" Kevin faked to the right, then grabbed Melanie as she scooted to the left. "Got you!"

Even ordinary peanut butter and jelly sandwiches tasted good on a picnic. Popcorn, too. Especially when they took turns seeing how high they could toss it before catching the buttery kernels in their mouths.

"Open wide," Dylan said, getting ready to pitch one to Christina. The first one missed, so she picked it up and tossed it to the birds. The second almost went the same way, but at the last second, she caught it with her tongue.

"I'm stuffed," Melanie said when the popcorn and sandwiches were all gone. She climbed to a flat rock and stretched out in the sun.

Christina followed, but instead of sunbathing, she pulled off her socks and sneakers and wiggled forward until her toes disappeared under the water. "Feels good," she said. "Are there any more cookies?"

Kevin held up the Ziploc bag that she and Melanie had filled the night before. There were only a few left.

"Catch," he said, tossing her one. Even though Kevin was the skinniest one there, he had already eaten two peanut butter and jelly sandwiches and most of the cookies.

"Who put you in charge of distribution?" Dylan said, laughing as he sat down next to Christina.

Katie was over by Bree, feeding her the last of her apple.

"I don't know about you," Chad said behind them. "But I'm ready to swing." He started climbing along the rocks to where the Tarzan rope hung off a huge tree growing between the rocks at the edge of the cliff.

"Didn't your mother ever tell you not to go swimming right after you eat?" Katie said in a joking voice. She climbed up to watch.

No way was Christina going to swing. She didn't even use the Tarzan rope at camp, and that one was a lot lower. Dylan jumped up to follow Chad.

"Do you think it's deep enough?" Christina asked him.

Dylan walked closer to the edge to check out the river. "Sure. That's why there's a rope." He dragged a dead sapling over, though, and fed one end of it down into the water until he got to the end of the tree. When he dragged it back out again, at least twelve feet of the stick was wet.

"What's the matter? You chicken?" Chad said, tugging on the rope. It was about an inch thick.

"No," Dylan said, coming up beside him. "Just

making sure the river is high enough." He squinted into the tree.

"I hope he doesn't crack his head open," Melanie said.

"Chad's head is as hard as a rock," Katie said, plopping down beside them.

Melanie laughed. "I meant Dylan."

"Here goes." Chad ran down the rock, picking his feet up at the edge and sailing out over the water. "Aaaaaaa—Aaaaaaaaa—Aaaaaaaa."

"Him, Tarzan. You, Jane," Melanie said to Katie.

Instead of dropping into the water, Chad rode the rope back.

"What's the matter? Chicken?" Kevin yelled, mimicking Chad.

"Naw. I was just testing it." Chad moved his hands further up the rope. He looked down at the water like he wasn't really sure he wanted to go in.

Christina stood up. The river was cloudy and still in the sunlight. "Be careful," she called as Chad started backing up for another try.

Chad didn't pay any attention. He took a deep breath, then ran down the rocks again. "Aaaaaaa—Aaaaaaaa—"

This time, the rest of his yell was swallowed by a splash. Dylan caught the empty rope as the circles where Chad disappeared got wider and wider.

Christina crept closer to the bank. Katie joined her as the seconds ticked by. "Do you think he's okay?"

Katie asked, looking worried.

Just then, the water erupted as Chad's head bobbed up, at least fifteen feet downstream from where he went in.

"Come on in, Becker. The water's great!"

Christina wished Dylan wouldn't. Something about disappearing under the cloudy water that way gave her the willies.

Dylan looked from the rope in his hand to the water.

"What are you waiting for?" Chad swam toward the bank.

Dylan backed up with the rope and ran. Christina didn't breathe when he swung out in space, letting go of the rope just in time to tuck into a cannonball before disappearing into the river. Her blood pounded in her ears like a clock ticking until she saw his head finally pop out of the water. He shook the hair out of his face and yelled, "Awesome. Come on, McLean. You gotta try it."

"No thanks," Kevin said, stuffing the trash into Melanie's backpack.

They all went in swimming, but Chad and Dylan were the only ones who used the swing. The last time Chad dropped from the rope, he came up under Katie, who giggled as she was lifted into the air on his shoulders.

"Chicken fights!" Dylan called out before disappearing under. A second later, Christina was rocketed out of the water.

"Dylan," she shouted, grabbing under his chin to hold on. "Put me down."

She half-giggled, half-screamed as she tried to keep from falling. "Dylan!"

After ignoring her at first, he finally ducked back down so she could get off.

"Didn't you hear me?" she said when she was safely on her own feet again in the water. She hated the way Dylan was showing off.

"Sorry. I thought you were having fun." Dylan looked honestly confused.

"You okay?" Katie called.

"I just don't like being that high up with nothing to hold on to," Christina explained, a little embarrassed to have made such a fuss.

"Come on, you guys," Kevin said with Melanie on his shoulders as he headed for Chad and Katie.

"Geronimo!" Melanie shouted, leaning out to push them over. Chad and Katie disappeared under water. They came up separately, laughing.

"This is war," Chad declared as Katie jumped onto his back.

Christina crossed her arms over her chest as she watched the four of them playing keep-away in the water. Dylan broke the silence.

"Friends?" Dylan asked.

Christina sighed. "Yeah, I guess."

"I'm sorry I scared you."

"That's okay," she said, feeling better. She went

around behind him and put her hands on his shoulders. "Let's go."

Dylan hoisted her onto his back and rushed the others. "Charge!"

Monday's riding lesson wasn't until after dinner. Melanie begged off since her shoulders hurt from getting sunburned at the river.

"I told you to use more lotion when you went swimming," Christina said as she gently rubbed some cool, green aloe gel into her cousin's tender skin. She had learned about sunburns the hard way with her freckled skin.

"I did. If Chad hadn't started the chicken fights, it wouldn't have washed off so fast." Melanie winced as she put her tank top strap back into place.

"It was fun, though," Christina said, remembering how she'd laughed so hard that Dylan had to hold her legs closer so she wouldn't fall off his back. Kevin and Mel had gotten dumped the most because they were smaller.

"Easy for you to say. Chad wasn't picking on you and Dylan. I'm sick of him flexing his muscles in my face."

Christina agreed. "I don't know what it is about some guys, always needing to prove how strong they are. I'm glad Dylan's not like that."

Melanie looked at Christina out of the corner of her

eyes. "He was acting pretty macho, too, if you ask me."

Christina thought about what Melanie said as she headed to the barn to get Sterling ready for the lesson. Dylan was only show-offish when Chad was around. He never acted that way with just her.

"Did you think we'd forgotten to turn you out?" Christina said as she led Sterling from her stall to the cross-ties. During the summer months when the horses spent the hottest daytime hours in the barn, they were turned outside to graze through the night.

"We're going for a dressage lesson at Mona's," Christina told her. "Then you can go out and play." She let Sterling nuzzle her cheek before turning to grab a brush.

First, the rubber curry comb. Christina started just below Sterling's ears with a series of circles that brought dust and dirt to the surface. Stopping every minute or so to knock the dirt from the brush, Christina worked her way down one side.

"You are such a dust magnet," she said, stopping to kiss the pinkish white snip on Sterling's nose before starting on the other side.

By the time she'd used the soft body brush to take off the final layer of dirt, Sterling's dapples were like pools of silver that darkened to pewter, then ebony on her legs, tail, and mane. Christina loved the way the mare's ears were outlined in black that matched her well-set eyes.

After Christina finished tacking up, she glanced at

her watch. Fifteen minutes to get there. That was plenty of time.

As they walked through the woods to Gardener Farm, Christina did a countdown to the event less than two weeks away. Two lessons this week, two the next, and the event was on Saturday and Sunday of the second week. In between lessons, she had to keep conditioning Sterling with gallops and long hacks, to say nothing of practicing whatever homework Mona gave them in dressage or jumping.

Katie was already in the new dressage ring Mona had marked off with a low white chain on the far side of the jumping arena. She was practicing riding past the trailer Mona had backed up by the C end. If this were a show, the judge and scribe—the person who writes down the judge's comments during a dressage test—would be sitting at a card table in the trailer. Most horses needed to look over the judge's area before settling down to the serious work of dressage.

"Where's Dylan?" Christina asked as she glanced back at the barn. Usually he was ready before she was.

"I don't think he's coming," Katie said. "Dakota's been turned out."

Sure enough, the big chestnut was grazing with a black gelding in the field. Christina sank a little in the saddle.

"Okay, girls. Let's start with a working trot," Mona said before she even reached the ring. "Since there's only two of you tonight, I'll have time to watch your dressage tests at the end of the lesson. You *do* have them memorized, don't you?"

"Why isn't Dylan riding?" Christina asked as she rode a twenty meter circle around Mona.

"Dakota pulled a shoe off last night," Mona said. "And the blacksmith can't get here until tomorrow. Now slow Sterling's rhythm and use more leg to open up her stride."

Christina squeezed her legs against Sterling's sides as she closed her fingers on the reins so Sterling would know to make her strides longer instead of faster. She tried to stay a fraction of a second longer in the saddle as she posted so Sterling would match her rhythm instead of vice versa. Sterling responded by lifting her back and settling into a nice dressage frame with her neck round and her nose perpendicular to the ground. "Good girl," Christina whispered, letting her inside hand creep forward for a second as she scratched Sterling's neck.

"Much nicer. If you keep this up, she'll be ready to move up to first level in dressage this fall," Mona said before turning her attention to Katie. "Seabreeze is too sluggish. Get her in front of your leg."

First level. First level. Her seat rose and fell softly in the saddle to Mona's words as Sterling mouthed the bit, waiting for her next command. It was all Christina could do to keep from shouting. The reading, the riding, the videos, and the lessons she'd been reliving in her head, they were all paying off—finally! She and Sterling were on their way.

*   *   *

"Chr-is. Telephone!" Melanie yelled from the porch as Christina turned Sterling out with the other horses after the lesson.

Christine waved. "I'll get it in the barn." She fastened the gate and jogged back to the tack room with Sterling's halter and lead line dangling from one hand. "Hello?"

"Hey." Dylan's voice was smooth and soft in her ear. "Did you have a good lesson?"

Christina hung up the halter, then shoved some galloping boots off her tack truck and climbed up. "Yeah. And except for shying once at the judge's trailer and breaking into a jig during the free walk, Sterling had a really good dressage test, too. Mona said we're almost ready to go first level."

"Coming from Mona, that's good."

Christina started to sit cross-legged, but her tall boots dug into the backs of her knees. She propped one foot up on the doorjamb, instead, as she got comfortable. "I heard Dakota threw a shoe."

"Yeah."

"You should have called. Our farrier was here this morning. If you had brought Dakota over, he would have tacked the shoe back on for you."

"I didn't think about that. I figured it could wait until tomorrow. Hey, cut it out."

Christina could hear fooling around in the background. "What's going on?" she asked, laughing.

"Hi, Christina." Chad's voice was all sing-songy.

Christina sighed. "Hi, Chad."

"Dylan wants to know if you like—"

Chad's voice cut off with a grunt and it sounded like the phone receiver fell. Christina twisted the long phone cord around her knee as she waited.

Dylan came back first. "You still there?"

Christina laughed. "What were you two *doing?*"

"Nothing." Chad started talking in the background again, but Dylan must have put his hand over the mouthpiece because everything got muffled.

"Sorry I didn't get to see you this afternoon," she said, smiling as she pictured his crooked grin.

"I was going to come and watch," Dylan said, "but then Chad showed up and we decided to get pizza instead. Hey, I saw an ad on the bulletin board for a rebuilt dirt bike for eight hundred dollars. Only the guy won't be home until nine, so I'm killing time until I can call back."

"Great," Christina said, trying to sound a little enthusiastic for Dylan's sake. "So, are you going to ride tomorrow?"

"Yeah, I guess, if the blacksmith comes in time. But I might have to check out that bike."

"You'd better ride," Christina said, only half-teasing. "The event is twelve days away."

Something beeped in Christina's ear. "Sorry," Dylan said after another noisy struggle at his end.

"That was Chad's watch. He set the alarm for nine o'clock."

Christina waited.

"I guess I'd better go so I can call this guy."

"Okay," Christina said.

"Well, good-bye. Hey—"

The phone went dead, probably because Chad grabbed it away.

Christina's arm felt heavy as she hung up the receiver. She was disappointed that Dylan hadn't said anything about riding with her tomorrow. His mind was definitely more on the dirt bike than horses.

If only he and Chad weren't getting to be such big buddies.

6

"I THINK YOU NEED TO CUT HIM SOME SLACK," KEVIN SAID after Christina finished complaining about Dylan. It was Wednesday afternoon, and she was annoyed because Dylan was too busy to ride with her today, too, even though he was the one who'd been gung-ho about training together.

"Yeah," Melanie agreed. "You don't want to act like you own him or anything."

Christina was glad Missy chose that second to shy at a big weed beside the road that was waving in the breeze like a hand. Her cheeks were hot as she circled the weanling, using her voice to coax her forward again. Terry, the little bay Melanie was leading, had hardly tossed her fuzzy black mane in the commotion, but Rascal, Kevin's weanling, was looking out of the corner of his eyes as he walked on tiptoe past the plant.

"Missy," Kevin said, "Rascal didn't even think twice about that leaf until you started acting dumb."

"She's not dumb," Christina said. "She's just being careful, aren't you girl?" Her voice was soft and reassuring.

"Maybe someday she'll grow up to be big and brave like Sterling," Melanie teased.

"Thanks a lot," Christina said. "Maybe if you and Kevin could tear yourselves away from the racehorses and ride with me more often, Sterling would learn not to spook at every little thing."

"When soccer's over, I'll have more time," Kevin said.

Christina groaned. "I just wish that this all-star stuff had been earlier in the summer instead of right before the event."

"Stop worrying, Cuz. With all the work you've been putting in, I bet you'll walk away with a blue ribbon," Melanie said, draping her arm over Terry's back. The foal popped her hindquarters in a half-buck, then trotted ahead, her silver-dollar-sized hooves dancing in the grass beside the pavement.

"It's not that," Christina said, though she had to admit that a blue ribbon at a recognized event would probably be the most exciting thing that had ever happened to her—second to buying Sterling, of course. Missy tugged at her lead line, wanting to trot to catch up to Terry, but Christina held her back. "I just wish Dylan, Katie, and I could get ready for this event together."

They'd gotten to the end of the long barn driveway so Christina let Missy drop her head for a few mouthfuls of grass. Kevin and Melanie did the same.

"Let's face it," Melanie said. "Not everybody stays interested in horses. Especially boys."

"What about me?" Kevin said, pretending to be insulted.

"You don't count," Melanie said, bumping him with her hip. "Horses are in your blood. Christina's, too. But I bet Dylan quits riding as soon as he's old enough to get his driver's license."

Christina watched Missy spread her long front legs apart like a baby giraffe so she could reach the shorter blades of grass with her pint-sized neck. "He's already acting like a dirt bike's more exciting than Dakota," she said glumly.

Missy put up her head and watched as a jeep stopped in front of the white mailbox with the Whitebrook Farm sign hanging above it. The mail carrier stretched over the seat to put a handful of envelopes in the box, then waved at them before grinding the gears and pulling away.

"I wonder if there's a letter from Dad," Melanie said, pulling Terry's head up and walking to the mailbox. Uncle Will was making an effort to write more often after Melanie got so mad at him for not coming to Parents' Day at the Saddlebrook Event Camp.

It took three tries before the filly would stand her ground when Melanie opened the metal door.

"Bill, bill, bill, postcard!" Melanie stuck the mail under her arm as she squinted, trying to make out the writing. "Dad's coming for a visit," she said, grinning.

"Great!" Christina said. "When?"

"A week from Friday." Melanie wrinkled her nose. "He's bringing Susan, too."

Christina knew her cousin would have preferred having Uncle Will all to herself, but Christina couldn't help being curious about Susan.

"Who's Susan?" Kevin asked, trying to convince Rascal that the grass wasn't any better on the other side of the driveway.

"Dad's girlfriend. She's the legal representative for his company. They'll be coming back from a business trip."

"Oh. Anything for me?" Kevin asked, grabbing the letters out from under Melanie's arm. He sorted through, handing Christina a flyer before sticking the mail back where he got it.

"I don't want it," Melanie said. They passed it back and forth before Kevin gave up, laughing as he coaxed Rascal close enough to the mailbox to stick it back in.

"Hey. There's a Jumper Day this Sunday at Foxwood Acres," Christina said, waving the paper. "I'm sorry," she apologized as Missy scooted out of the way. She held the sheet out for Missy to sniff, snatching it back only when the weanling decided to see how it tasted.

"It will be a perfect warm-up for Sterling before the

event," Christina said. "You want to take Trib?"

Melanie shook her head. "I don't even want to think about putting on a hot, black riding coat before fall."

"You don't have to," Christina said. "It's just a schooling show. Everybody will be wearing breeches and polo shirts."

"I don't know, Cuz. The only jumping I feel like doing is into a pool."

Christina wrinkled her nose. "How about you, Kev?"

"I'm going to pass, too. Soccer's keeping me busy right now. We'll cheer you on, though," he added, grabbing Melanie around the waist. Terry put her ears back and lunged at Rascal.

"Watch it," Melanie said, laughing as she pulled away.

Christina hoped she could talk Dylan and Katie into showing, because it wouldn't be any fun by herself. Dylan will probably have soccer practice, though, which would mean that Katie would probably want to watch Chad instead of taking Bree to the show.

"Come on, girl." Christina clucked as she pulled Missy's head up from the grass and followed Melanie and Kevin back to the barn. She'd be glad when soccer was over so things could get back to normal again.

Dylan wasn't home on Wednesday night when Christina called, and Katie was baby-sitting, so Christina had to wait until the jumping lesson on Thursday afternoon to tell them about the Jumper Day show.

"Sure, I'd like to take Dakota, but I might have soccer practice." Dylan raised his stirrups to jumping length as he talked. "Chad said his father might want to scrimmage on Sunday, since the first all-star game is Monday."

"I don't know if I can go either," Katie said when Christina looked at her. "I want to talk to Chad first."

"Are you ready?" Mona called as she came out of the barn. "We're going to work on cross-country today, so bring the horses into the field."

Chad, Chad, Chad, Christina thought as she turned Sterling and started walking to where Mona was holding the gate open. Between Dylan and Katie talking about him all the time, Christina was getting sick of his name.

Christina called Katie on Saturday afternoon to see if she had decided yet about the Jumper Day show.

"Didn't Dylan tell you?" Katie said. "Mr. Walker is giving the team Sunday off. We're all coming. Chad, too."

"Great!" Christina said, wondering why Dylan hadn't called to tell her. Oh, well. The important thing was that the three of them would get to show.

Christina only half-listened as Katie talked about going for ice cream with the team after practice. "You should come to soccer again. I know Dylan likes it when you're there."

"I'll go to the all-star games with you," Christina promised. She missed seeing her two best friends.

Sunday was hot and buggy as Dylan, Katie, and Christina walked in the shade along the sandy shoulder of River Road. The nice thing about Foxwood Acres was that it was close enough to ride to instead of going in the trailer.

"It doesn't even feel like we're showing," Katie said. "Usually I have lots of butterflies in my stomach."

Dylan looked relaxed, too, as he brushed a deerfly away from Dakota's neck with his bat. "And I'm glad I don't have to wear a stupid tie," he added.

They were all in polo shirts, breeches, and boots since the Jumper Day was a schooling show where nobody was expected to dress up or braid their horses' manes. Christina had ridden Trib in the show once, but this was the first time she had taken Sterling.

"It's too bad Melanie and Kevin aren't also showing," Katie said.

"They're going to ride over on their bikes, though, as soon as they're finished working the racehorses." Christina glanced at her watch as they turned up the driveway to Foxwood Acres. Even though it wasn't eight o'clock yet, the field beside the white-fenced show ring was buzzing with activity. Sterling felt two inches taller when she quickened her pace and whinnied to the horses being led around by riders of all ages.

"Good morning, everyone." A cheerful male voice came out of the speaker above the ring.

"Class number one, junior jumpers in the two-foot three-inches division, will begin in fifteen minutes."

Christina, Dylan, and Katie each signed up for two classes in the three-foot division. After slipping the numbered pinnies over their shirts, they stopped at the refreshment table inside the indoor arena and bought doughnuts and juice for themselves and a carrot for each of the horses.

"It's going to turn their mouths orange," Katie said as she loosened Bree's noseband so the mare could chew more comfortably.

"I don't care," Christina said, scratching Sterling behind her ears. "All the judge is going to be looking for are knockdowns or refusals. We're here to have fun, aren't we, cutie?" She planted a kiss on Sterling's silky nose.

They headed for a shady spot on the far side of the ring where they could watch the jumping. Sterling was so busy looking around, she wouldn't stand still.

"I hope Chad gets here before I ride," Kate said.

I hope he leaves his dirt bike home, Christina added silently.

By the time the two-foot six-inches division started, the sun was hot and Christina was starting to wonder if Melanie and Kevin had decided to go swimming instead of coming to the show. Water would feel pretty good right now.

"Hey, Chad. Over here," Katie called, waving.

Chad was walking his dirt bike across the grass with Kevin and Melanie right behind him with their mountain bikes.

"Man," Chad complained as he skirted a pile of manure. "It's like a minefield around here."

"Have you gone yet?" Kevin asked Dylan.

"No. There's still one more class before ours."

Chad parked his dirt bike well away from where the horses were milling. He grinned at Dylan as he walked up.

"Hey, Becker. Are you sure you're supposed to be here? I don't see any other guys in tights."

Dylan laughed. "You're just jealous you're not the one surrounded by girls."

"Maybe you're right." When Chad stuck his hands in his back pockets and checked out the scenery, Katie leaned off Bree and whacked him on the head. "Ow!"

"Want a soda?" Melanie pulled a can out of her backpack and held it up to Christina.

"Just a swig," she said. "I want to start warming up Sterling."

"What's the big deal?" Chad said. "I could walk over those jumps."

"We all could, Chad," Melanie said, rolling her eyes at Christina. "The trick is to do it on a horse."

It took three times around the field before Sterling

relaxed and started listening to her. Christina was so busy concentrating that she didn't notice Dylan ride up until Sterling whinnied "hello."

"They're setting up for our class now," Dylan said, trotting alongside. Sterling swished her tail and pinned her ears back, making it clear that Dakota was invading her space. "Sorry," Dylan said, widening the gap between them.

"I don't know what her problem is today." Christina sat deep in the saddle and closed her hands on the reins so Sterling would walk.

"Probably just full of herself." Dylan walked Dakota, too, but Sterling didn't fuss at him this time as they stayed shoulder to shoulder. "You've gotten her pretty fit."

"How's Dakota?" Christina asked. "I've hardly seen you guys lately."

"Tell me about it." Dylan frowned. "I've had to drop his girth down a hole. If I don't get back to riding him more often, he's going to look like Pork Chop."

Pork Chop was a horse at event camp who was as round as a sausage. "Poor Dakota. First you ignore him, then you insult him," Christina said, only half-teasing.

Kevin and Melanie offered to hold onto the horses while Dylan and Christina walked the course. Chad cut out to the refreshment stand before Katie could ask him to take Bree, so Kevin ended up holding two horses.

The course was pretty straightforward with only two jumps that worried Christina. One was the Liverpool, which would be an ordinary enough fence if it weren't for the shallow, plywood box in front of it that was painted blue to look like water. Sterling had taken a dislike to the Liverpool at Mona's. Christina didn't like it much, either, since that was the jump where she had fallen and broken her wrist earlier this summer.

Stop that, she told herself. Sterling had been jumping the Liverpool fine lately. If she worried about it, the mare would sense it and refuse to jump. Christina knew how important it was for her to think positively, since Sterling could almost read her mind sometimes.

The other jump that she'd have to be especially careful about was the fence that looked like a railroad crossing. It was only four-feet wide, instead of the usual ten, so Sterling would have to jump it right in the middle. If she drifted off to the sides, Christina's riding boot could run into the standard.

"Are you going to ride four strides or five strides between the wall and the barrels?" Dylan asked as they walked back to the horses. His arm was warm when it brushed up against hers.

"I'm going to try for five strides," Christina answered. "I'm afraid if I push her to take it in four, she'll get too excited and run. And I don't want to give her any excuse to quit at the barrels again."

"I don't care how many strides Bree puts in, as long

as she'll jump it," Katie said. "She's so sluggish in this heat, I may have to use my bat to get her engine running."

Christina laughed. "Engine running? You've been hanging around Chad too much."

By the time Sterling went over the third practice fence in the warm-up area, the mare was so fired up she was taking off a stride too soon and jumping twice as high as she needed.

"Now *that's* a horse," Chad said. "How come you can't make Dakota jump like that?"

"You don't want a horse to jump like this," Christina said as she cantered by. "It's dangerous." She'd seen horses flip over bigger fences when they misjudged the distance and took off too soon.

There were nine horses in their division. Christina was going fourth, with Katie and Dylan immediately following her. They stood outside the ring to watch while they waited their turns.

The first horse and rider swept too wide after the red-and-white oxer and ended up running out at the narrow railroad-crossing jump. They jumped it the second time, but the first refusal had left them with ten penalty points. "I should have trotted," the girl said, shaking her head as they left the ring.

The second horse's round wasn't bad until he knocked a rail off the barrels and was left with five penalty points.

The third horse went around so fast that when he

refused at the wall, the rider shot over his head and ended up standing on the other side, holding the reins and looking dazed.

I hope I don't do that, Christina thought as she gathered up her reins to go in.

"The next horse is Sterling Dream, owned and ridden by Christina Reese."

Christina closed her leg on Sterling's sides and smiled as the mare responded with a floating trot.

"Go, Chris," Melanie shouted as Christina halted in front of the judge and saluted.

"Okay, girl. Let's do it." Christina sank deep into the saddle as she asked for a canter, her head turned toward the first fence as they circled. She could feel Sterling looking around, eager to know which jump to take. When Christina steered her between the two starting flags to the jump with the flower pots, Sterling's ears flicked back once, then stayed forward as she closed the gap.

Three, two, now, Christina counted as Sterling met the first fence perfectly and sailed over without touching a rail. Before they even landed, Christina looked for the second jump, a white coop with two plastic dwarfs on either side. Sterling hesitated as she took in the strange sight, but Christina dropped back in the saddle and urged her over with inches to spare.

Sterling's hind foot knocked the railing of the second part of the in-and-out—a two-jump obstacle with just enough room for them to canter one stride between. Christina couldn't glance over her shoulder to see if a rail was on the ground, though, because Sterling was picking up speed.

"Easy, girl," Christina said, riding a series of half-halts to try to get Sterling back into balance again. Sterling was too busy shying away from the barrels to listen. "We're not even jumping them yet," Christina hissed as she used every ounce of leg she had to bend Sterling toward the Liverpool. Fortunately, Sterling sailed over, hardly even looking at the "water" underneath.

They weren't even halfway through the course and Christina felt like her arms were about to break off. "Whoa," she said, firmly bringing Sterling back to a trot before they circled to the left to approach the narrow train-crossing obstacle. She needed to get Sterling reorganized.

At least trotting to the narrow fence gave Sterling plenty of time to look at it. Christina made a wall with her legs and hands, refusing to let Sterling go anywhere but forward. The mare hesitated a fraction of a second before popping over the yellow-and-black striped gate and quietly cantering to the blue-and-white spread. They cleared that without a problem and Christina heard her friends cheering them on.

The rest of the course was smooth and steady. Christina loved the way Sterling blew through her nose, punctuating every stride. The mare's head was up and her ears pricked as she carried Christina over the brightly colored fences. Even the red, white, and blue barrels didn't pose any real problems, unless she counted the three flying changes of lead that Sterling did as she approached the jump. When she bunched up her muscles and flew over the last jump, a plywood ramp with a fox's head and FOXWOOD ACRES painted in maroon and white across the front, Sterling felt like she was game to do all ten fences again.

"That was a clear round for number thirty-six, Sterling Dream," the announcer said. "Next horse is number thirty-seven, Seabreeze—owned and ridden by Katie Garrity."

"Good luck, Katie!" Christina said as she brought Sterling back to a walk and waited to go out of the gate.

"Thanks." Katie's face was flushed as she nudged Bree into a trot.

"Did he say Sterling went clean?" Christina asked Dylan as she left the ring.

"Yeah." Dylan held his hand up for a high five. "Congratulations."

Christina leaned forward to give Sterling a pat. "I thought for sure we'd pulled a rail at the in-and-out."

"That pole jumped four inches up and landed right back in the holder cup," Melanie said. "You were lucky, Cuz."

Chad stuck his fingers in his mouth and whistled as Katie started toward the first fence. Christina watched as she walked to cool Sterling off.

It was a good round until the last fence. Christina groaned as Bree hit the pole with her hind leg and it dropped to the ground.

"That was too bad," she said as she met Katie at the gate. "You rode a nice, quiet course."

Katie was philosophical. "Too quiet. I should have woken her up after she touched the panels."

"Loverboy's in," Chad said.

Christina found a place on the railing where she and Sterling could watch.

Dakota's chestnut coat was burnished to a coppery sheen. Dylan looked confident as he jumped the first fence, his head already turned and looking toward the next one. He and Dakota were well-matched as they jumped the course without a hitch—a perfect mix of strength and grace. Dakota's front feet had hardly hit the ground after the last fence before Dylan was leaning forward, slapping his neck with praise as they cantered through the finish flags.

"That was number thirty-eight, Dakota. A clean round by Dylan Becker."

"That was great," Christina said.

"He was all business. Man, I love this horse." Dylan's eyes shone as he patted Dakota again.

Chad guffawed and shook his head as he sauntered over holding up a can of soda. "Better take a swig of this before you ask him to go steady. I think the sun's frying your brain."

"Shut up, Chad," Christina said.

"Got to watch it," Chad said in a whisper, nudging Dylan's boot with his shoulder. "I think you're making her jealous."

Dylan rolled his eyes, but he was laughing as he swung off Dakota's back.

Christina, Dylan, and a girl riding an Arab all had clear rounds, so they had to ride in a jump-off to break the tie. Christina worried as she watched the ground crew prop poles in front of the fences that weren't going to be used. The jump-off was going to be timed, so if she wanted to do well, they'd have to go fast. And Sterling already had a problem with racing over fences.

The jump-off round only had five fences. It was a snaky course where the horses would have to change direction after every fence. A timer with a stopwatch around his neck stood by the start flags, which would also serve as the finish flags for this round. The horse with no jumping faults and the fastest time would win.

"Of course, Dakota has the advantage, being a Quarter Horse and all."

Christina started to get her back up before she saw the twinkle in Dylan's eyes. "Oh yeah? Dakota might be bred for short races and quick turns, but in a *real* race, Sterling would leave him in her dust." She made a "so there!" face at Dylan before laughing and picking up her reins. "Come on, Sterling. Let's show him what a *Thoroughbred* can do."

Sterling was keen as they entered the ring again.

Her feet hovered in the air for a second before coming down as she trotted. *Her tail was probably halfway up in a flag,* Christina thought as they stopped to salute.

When Sterling leaped into a canter from their halt, Christina started having second thoughts about trying to have the fastest time. Sure she might get a ribbon, but it wouldn't be worth it if Sterling went away from the show thinking it was okay to blast her way around a stadium course.

"Steady, girl," Christina said, her seat almost touching the saddle as she tried to keep Sterling from charging the panels. They ended up coming in too close and Sterling had to twist in the air to clear the jump without her back feet hitting the wood. She squealed and tried to get her head down to buck as soon as she landed. Christina was so busy getting her to slow and rebalance, that she overshot the turn for the next jump and ended up coming into it at too much of an angle. Sterling leaped over the rails with more determination than style.

"That's it," Christina said, pulling her back. "If you won't listen to me at a canter, then we'll just have to trot." The jumps weren't any higher than the gymnastics Mona made them trot over, so she knew Sterling could do it. The mare's ears were pinned as Christina insisted she ride between the fences politely, but she used her back correctly over each jump and they finished with a clean, if slow, round.

The girl on the Arab went next. The turns weren't a

problem with her short-strided canter and in less than a minute, she went through the finish flags with no jumping faults.

"Good luck," Christina said as Dylan rode by.

"Yeah. Don't let a couple of girls beat you," Chad said, followed by an "Ow!" when Katie stuck her elbow in his ribs. "I was just kidding."

Christina laughed. Chad was hopeless.

She was surprised when Dylan shot through the starting flags in a hand gallop. He was already turning Dakota's head to the left in midair over the first jump. Sand flew up as they carved a sharp turn and took the second fence at the same quick pace.

Too quick, in Christina's opinion. Dakota was barely handling the turns and she was afraid they would slip if he didn't slow down.

They were going so fast after the third fence that Dylan missed his shortcut to the fourth fence—the railroad-crossing gate. He circled around the stone wall and headed to the narrow fence at too sharp an angle. Dakota wavered as though he was going to run out, but Dylan held firm and forced him over. As they jumped the yellow-and-black gate, the toe of Dylan's boot caught the standard, tipping it forward under Dakota.

The heavy, black standard hit Dakota's back leg just below the stifle—the place where his leg connected to his hindquarters. Christina's knee hurt empathetically as she watched Dakota take a couple of three-legged, painful strides before he put his full weight on the leg again and cantered toward the last fence. Christina was afraid Dylan was going to jump it, but at the last second, he circled Dakota away, waving to the judge that he was retiring from the class.

"Is Dakota okay?" Christina said, dismounting.

"I think so." Dylan dropped his stirrups and slid to the ground. He felt along the dimpled stifle joint.

"Man, you had it made before you hit that jump," Chad said, coming up. "If your big foot hadn't gotten in the way, you could have won that class." He shook his head, laughing.

Christina frowned. "It's not funny, Chad."

"Cool it," Dylan said to Christina. "Dakota's fine." He turned to Chad. "You want to come with me to look at that bike again? I might sound out the guy to see if he'll take seven hundred."

Christina stared at Dylan's profile. She couldn't believe he was just brushing the whole thing off like that. "How do you know he's fine?"

Dylan turned, but not before Christina glimpsed the exasperated look he exchanged with Chad. "Look. When I bang my leg in soccer, I limp for a few steps. He bangs his leg, he limps." Dylan lowered his voice so she could barely hear it. "Don't make a federal case out of it. Okay?"

"But it was dangerous the way you took that jump," she said, lowering her voice to match his. "Why were you riding him so fast, anyway?"

Dylan shook his head. "You don't understand."

Christina frowned. "You're right. I don't understand." As she turned to get back on Sterling, her name was called for second place.

"Yay, Chris!" Melanie, Katie, and Kevin called.

"Good girl," Christina said, leaning forward to pat Sterling as she rode into the arena to accept her award. She was still grinning when she came out of the ring—until she looked around.

Dylan and Chad were gone.

7

"YOU PROBABLY SHOULDN'T HAVE CRITICIZED HIM IN FRONT of everyone," Melanie pointed out Sunday night.

"I didn't do it front of everyone. Besides, it was stupid to come into the gate so fast," Christina said as she rinsed the frying pan from dinner and passed it to Melanie to dry. "He was just trying to act like a hotshot in front of Chad."

"And you've never shown off before?" Melanie bumped Christina's hip with hers. "Just call and say you're wondering how Dakota is."

"After he left without saying good-bye? No thanks."

"I bet he was just mad about blowing the class." She reached across Christina to grab a sponge for wiping the counters. "And it was probably smart of him to give Dakota the rest of the day off after getting banged like that."

Christina's sigh was so big it rustled the curtains over the sink. "I don't see how Dylan can take Chad putting him down all the time because he rides."

Melanie shrugged. "You're making too big a deal out of it. Boys insult each other all the time."

"Wait a minute," Christina said, turning off the faucet and drying her hands on her shorts. "Since when did you become such an authority on boys?"

"You don't see Kevin and me fighting all the time, do you?" Melanie said, pretending to slap Christina's leg with the dish towel.

By the time Christina got the sponge wet enough to throw, Melanie was already halfway up the stairs. She was about to chase her up when the phone rang. It was Dylan.

"So, how did you do in the second class?" he asked after saying "hi."

"Fourth place. We dropped a rail." Christina paused. "How's Dakota?"

"He's fine." Dylan cleared his throat. "Hey, I'm sorry I left like that."

"That's okay," Christina said. "I'm sorry I was telling you how to ride."

"Yeah, well, you were right. I *was* going too fast."

"But I shouldn't have said anything."

"Forget it," Dylan said.

Ashleigh stuck her head in the kitchen. "Almost done? I have a call to make."

Christina nodded. "I've got to go."

"Hey. Do you want to watch our game tomorrow? It's at home, against Northfield."

"Sure. What time?"

"Ten. And maybe we can ride when it's over." Dylan's voice was hopeful.

"Okay."

"Great. I'll see you then."

Christina took the stairs two at a time to tell Melanie.

A lot of people turned out for the game, considering it was on a weekday.

"Hi," Christina called, waving to Dylan's mother before sitting in the grass at Dylan's end of the field. She wished she had brought a hat to shade her eyes.

"Don't they look great in their uniforms?" Katie said, poking her with an elbow.

The team did look good in their baggy shorts and bright red shirts with ANGELENO'S ANGELS written in yellow script letters across the back. Mr. Walker had talked Angeleno's Pizza Parlor into buying the shirts. Dylan saw her and waved with a great big smile on his face. When the first ball went into play, though, he was all business.

Northfield's team was strong, and for the first half of the game Dylan spent most of his time directing the fullbacks and defending the goal. When he leaped up and deflected a ball that Christina had been certain was going into the net, everyone jumped to their feet and Melanie whistled.

Dylan's reflexes amazed Christina, especially the way he could catch the ball and drop-kick it almost in a single movement. The game was so fast that Christina wondered how long Dylan and the fullbacks could hold up against the pressure.

"Come on, Chad," Katie shouted when Dylan sent the ball up the field to him. Christina thought the Northfield center was going to get it first, but Chad leaped in front of him, heading the ball to Kevin who took it up the sidelines.

"Go, go!" Christina was screaming so loud her throat hurt. Kevin passed the ball back to Chad, who shot it into the goal a split second before the airhorn went off, signaling the end of the first half.

"Wow," Christina said to Katie and Melanie after they'd finished jumping around and hugging each other. "I'm exhausted." She couldn't imagine how the players must feel.

When the game ended, Angeleno's Angels had scored three goals to Northfield's one.

"We're going to be the county champs," Chad gloated as he, Dylan, and Kevin came over. Their shirts were plastered to their backs from a victory water-fight.

"It's only our first win," Kevin pointed out. "But man, what a game."

Dylan untucked his shirt from his shorts and used the hem to wipe his face. "I'm beat."

"You were fantastic," Christina said. "I couldn't believe it when you blocked that penalty kick."

"No thanks to you, Walker." Dylan gave Chad a fake punch on the arm. "The way you rammed into that guy, I thought you'd get thrown out of the game."

Chad shrugged. "What can I say? It's not my fault the county's too wimpy to have a rugby league."

"Come on, tough guy. I'm ready to swim." Katie grabbed Chad's shirt and pulled him away. "You guys coming?"

Kevin looked at Melanie. "Want to?"

"Sure. It's too hot to do anything else, anyway."

"Chris?" Dylan's eyebrows went up.

The thought of pulling on hot breeches wasn't nearly as appealing as the pool. "Oh, what the heck. The horses could probably use a day off, anyway."

Dylan grabbed her hand. "Great. Let's go!"

On Thursday morning, Melanie danced across the floor with an empty cereal bowl in her hand. "Only one more day."

"Two," Christina said, holding up two fingers without looking up from her *Practical Eventing* book.

Melanie put the bowl in the sink, then hoisted herself onto the counter. "One. Dad will be here tomorrow night."

"Oh," Christina said. "I thought you were talking about the event."

Melanie stuck a finger under her chin and tilted her head. "Event? What event?"

"The one where you were going to be my groom," Christina said, trying to look stern.

"I'll help you on Sunday if they leave in time," Melanie said. "And if someone will give me a ride over."

"Don't worry about it," Christina said. "With Dylan, Katie, and me going, we'll be able to help each other."

"Speaking of Dylan..." Melanie turned a chair around and straddled it like a horse. "How was your lesson yesterday?"

"Good," Christina said, remembering. Even though Dylan's third all-star game had been as grueling as the first two, Dylan still rode a great test at Mona's dressage lesson. Christina was impressed; she didn't know if she had that kind of stamina. "We're going to school-over jumps together at Mona's this morning."

"I thought your mom said Mona was going with her to Lexington?"

"She is. That's why we're just schooling instead of having a lesson. We'll help each other out."

"You're still coming to the soccer game with me this afternoon, aren't you?" Melanie asked.

"Sure," Christina said, trying not to think about all the stuff she had to clean before the event. "I can't duck out on the Angels when they're still undefeated."

Melanie grabbed a fuzzy peach from the basket on the table and jumped up to wash it. "What's Dylan going to do about the event if they make it to the play-offs on Saturday?"

"I don't know," Christina said. "Hope that the game won't be scheduled for the same time as his dressage test. We should be getting our dressage and cross-country starting times in the mail today." Dylan didn't sound worried when she asked him that same question yesterday, but Christina still wondered if he could pull it off.

Mona was just heading out in her red truck when Christina rode into Gardener Farm. The riding teacher's neatly pressed khaki pants and shirt looked out-of-place as she opened the truck door and leaned out, calling to Christina. "I've already told the others not to jump the horses' socks off," she said. "You don't want to over-school two days before the event."

"We won't," Christina assured her, smiling as she noticed that in spite of the going-to-town clothes, Mona's short brown hair was as tousled as always.

"Good. Sarah had to go to the university to register for the fall semester this morning, but Matt is here if you need him."

Christina nodded, a little disappointed that Sarah Hale, the part-time groom who also taught beginner lessons at Gardener Farm, wouldn't be around to watch. She always had something nice to say about Sterling.

Dylan was still tacking up Dakota when Christina got off Sterling and led her into the wide-aisled barn. "I spent the morning setting up a new course," he said, lifting the flap of his saddle. Dakota pinned his ears back and made an ugly face in Dylan's direction as he tightened the girth. "Go check it out."

Katie was already in the ring, letting Bree look at the fences. Christina noticed Dylan had included one narrow jump using some of the broken poles.

"Have you jumped, yet?" Christina asked, noticing Bree had already broken out in a sweat on her neck and flanks.

"No. I was working on dressage while I waited for you."

By the time Dylan warmed up, Katie and Christina had gone over all the fences once and were making up a course for each other. "Has Dylan jumped Dakota since Sunday?" Christina asked in a low voice. She wondered if the fence falling on him had caused any problems.

"I don't think so," Katie answered.

Christina's fears were laid to rest when Dakota jumped the cross-rails and the oxer in his usual good form.

"Put more weight in your heels," Katie said, mimicking Mona perfectly. "And keep your eyes up."

Dylan laughed as he turned and headed to the coop. Dakota jumped it like it wasn't even there.

"Well done," Christina said in her best, English

accent. Dylan pretended to tip his hat as he cantered by and headed to the narrow vertical. He almost fell off when Dakota swerved to the right at the last second.

"Hey," Katie said, giggling. "Why don't you look where you're going?"

Dylan shook his head and patted Dakota's neck. "Sorry, buddy. I'll get serious now." He trotted a circle, picked up a canter halfway around, and approached the jump again. This time when Dakota started to run out, Dylan opened the opposite rein and kept him straight. Dakota put the brakes on, and slid into the rails, knocking them out of the cups.

"I'll get them," Christina said, swinging her leg over Sterling's saddle and sliding off.

Dakota backed away from the jump and tried to spin around.

"Whoa," Dylan said, making him stand.

"He's probably remembering the show," Christina said. Before Dylan could respond, Chad came up the Gardener Farm driveway on his dirt bike.

"Hi, Chad," Katie called.

Chad set the kickstand and walked over to the fence. "You almost done?"

Katie's eyes moved from Chad to the jumps, then back. "Maybe I will call it a day. Mona said not to jump them too much right before the event, anyway."

Chad raised his chin and called to Christina, "Did you hit the deck?"

"No." Christina was a little insulted that he

assumed she'd fallen off. "I'm fixing the jump Dakota knocked down. Do you want me to make it lower this time?" she said to Dylan.

"Naw. He should jump it the way it was."

"You call that little thing a jump?" Chad quipped. Katie was walking out of the ring, but instead of following her, Chad climbed onto the fence like he was ready for a performance.

"You've ridden once, so that makes you an authority?" Now that Christina knew Chad better, she liked giving him a hard time.

Dylan wasn't paying any attention to them. He circled Dakota at a canter, frowning with concentration as he headed again for the narrow fence. Dakota's ears flicked back and forth as they approached it, and Christina could see Dylan using a lot of leg to keep him cantering.

"Get up there," Dylan said, reaching back to slap Dakota on the rump with his bat. The chestnut leaped forward, his front feet actually leaving the ground as if he were going to jump. But at the last second, he dropped his shoulder and cut to the left, spilling Dylan in the process. Dakota reeled away as the poles—and Dylan—came crashing down.

"He got you good that time," Chad hooted from the fence.

Christina started to ask if Dylan was all right, but thought better of it when he sprang to his feet without even looking at them. He walked over to where

Dakota was standing and blowing as if he'd just finished a gallop.

"I think he's scared," Christina said as Dylan led
the chestnut back to the jump so he could fix the rails.
"He must think that it's going to fall down on him,
every time he gets close to a narrow jump."

"Well, he's got to learn." Dylan's voice was short.

At first, Dakota didn't even want to walk close to
the standards. Christina winced as Dylan jerked on the
reins, forcing Dakota on.

"Show him who's boss," Chad yelled.

"Shut up, Chad," Christina said. "Your yakking
isn't helping."

Dakota pulled back two more times as Dylan
started to lift a pole up.

"Want me to do that?" Chad offered from the fence.

"No." It was at least five minutes before Dakota
finally stood still long enough for Dylan to get the two
four-foot poles back into place. As soon as they were
up, Dylan remounted.

"Good boy," Christina called to Dakota, surprised
that Dylan wasn't fussing over him at all. "Why don't
you let him just stand and look at it a second?" she
suggested.

"You could get a carrot to dangle in front of him,"
Chad added. He was the only one who laughed at his
own joke.

Dylan didn't answer, but he let Dakota stretch
down and sniff while he fiddled with his stirrups. "No

more fooling around," Dylan said when he turned away and kicked Dakota into a trot. He smacked him with the bat once to let him know he meant business.

Mona's favorite saying ran through Christina's head, "When anger starts, learning stops." She wished the riding teacher was here to help.

Dylan had Dakota trotted into the fence, but Christina could tell from ten feet away that the chestnut had no intention of jumping. But this time, Dylan was ready when Dakota slid to a stop like a Western reining horse. He took the reins into one hand and started whacking Dakota on both sides of his hindquarters with the bat.

Dakota didn't know which way to run. Christina could see the white part of his eyes as he threw his head up in fright.

"You're . . . going . . . to . . . jump." Dylan's face was beet-red as the bat punctuated each word. Dakota, unable to turn either way to escape, finally reared. Dylan leaned forward, dropping his bat as he grabbed mane to keep from sliding off the back of the saddle. By the time Dakota came down and lunged away from the fence, Christina had trotted to the jump and vaulted off.

"He's too scared," she shouted, sweeping the bat off the ground.

"Here." Dylan swung Dakota back around and leaned over with his palm outstretched.

Christina closed her fingers tightly on the bat. "No.

Not while you're mad at him."

Dylan's eyes darted to Chad. "Come on, Chris," he said, with pain in his voice. "I can't let him get away with not jumping."

"But beating isn't going to help. It just makes him more afraid." She remembered how she'd lost her temper once and used the bat on Sterling when she wouldn't cross the creek. Her eyes watered at the memory.

"I'm not really hurting him. You know the bat is mostly just noise." Dylan rubbed Dakota's hair where the leather thong had parted it.

Chad came up beside them. "Don't you have one of those long whips like they use in a circus?" He turned when Christina gasped. "I'm not talking about *hitting* him with it. I bet if I cracked it behind him, he would jump."

Christina looked up at Dylan. "I think you should wait until Mona comes back so she can help."

Dylan picked up the reins. "I don't need her help. Besides, there isn't time. We've got to be at the soccer field by noon."

"How about if you let him follow Sterling over a couple of times to get his confidence back?" Christina said. She knew that Dakota would be a lot more likely to jump if Sterling went first.

"What am I supposed to do if he refuses at the event? Ask for a lead-over?" Dylan's voice was heavy with sarcasm.

Christina understood what it felt like to be so mad

and frustrated at the same time. Working with animals who had minds of their own sometimes made riding a tough sport, and Dylan of all people knew that. Christina couldn't remember ever seeing him lose his temper with a horse before. Why was he doing it now?

"Come on, Chris." Dylan's voice was impatient.

She made a quick decision. Still holding onto the bat, she swung up on Sterling.

"I think you're making a mistake bullying him," she said quietly, squeezing Sterling forward out of Dylan's reach. "And I don't want to watch you doing it."

She left the ring, pausing only long enough to toss the bat inside the barn door. As she turned Sterling toward the woods, she heard Dylan yelling at Dakota again. The trail blurred as she pushed Sterling into a trot. *What was going on with Dylan, anyway?*

8

CHRISTINA WAS UP TO HER ELBOWS IN SOAPSUDS ON FRIDAY when Uncle Will and Susan drove up in a navy blue BMW convertible with the top down. She and Sterling had gone for a hack in the morning, and now Christina was giving her a bath on the driveway in front of the barn so she'd be clean for the next day's event.

"Dad," Melanie called out, running and almost jumping into Uncle Will's arms. A tall woman with dark brown hair that swung against her jaw got out of the other side.

"Hi," Christina said, cupping her hands around her mouth. Uncle Will looked around a second before spotting her by the barn closest to the house and waved. *So this was Susan,* Christina thought, appraising the chic, cream-colored suit that accented her model-thin figure. She was too far away to hear the conversation, but Susan gave Melanie a hug and Uncle Will tugged her hair as they all walked to the house. Christina was happy to see them looking like a family. Maybe Uncle Will had finally fallen in love, and Melanie could have two parents again.

Even though she was glad things were going well for her cousin, Christina couldn't shake the bad feeling she had every time she thought about Dylan and Dakota's battle yesterday. She had hoped Dylan would have called last night, but he hadn't. She certainly wasn't going to call him.

"We're not going to let it spoil the event for us, are we, sweetie?" Christina said, rubbing the warm, sudsy sponge along Sterling's dapples.

"The wash stall's free, if you want it," Eddie Wilcox, one of Whitebrook's grooms, called.

"Thanks." Christina led Sterling into the three-sided concrete stall and turned her around so she could face the aisle. The mare stamped her foot against the thick, black rubber mat as Christina fastened the cross-ties to her halter. Getting a bath wasn't Sterling's favorite thing in the world, and the mare swished her wet tail against Christina's legs to let her know how she felt about being tied up during it.

"You want to fight dirty?" Christina said, lifting the soapy pail and moving to Sterling's hindquarters. "Two can play that game." She stuck Sterling's whole tail into the bucket, her fingers massaging the dirt out of the silver-streaked hair, then she used the hose to rinse it clean. Before Sterling could whip her again, she tucked the long, thick hairs safely into a mud knot.

"Pretty spiffy," her mother said.

Christina spun around. "I didn't even hear you come up."

"You were in your own little world," Ashleigh said, watching from the aisle. She made a face and tugged at the sundress she had put on for their company. "And frankly," she added. "I'd rather be standing where you are."

Christina understood completely. Even though she knew her mom was always glad to see Uncle Will, it was hard to interrupt the horses' schedules to entertain people.

"How much more time do you need before you can come up for lunch?" Ashleigh asked.

"Forty-five minutes?" After shampooing Sterling, she had to rinse her with bluing to make her coat brighter, then hand-graze her until she was dry enough to go back into the stall.

"I'll put the chicken salad out in a hour," Ashleigh said, giving her the once-over. "That should leave you enough time to change and wash up."

"What's to wash?"

Ashleigh laughed as Christina held out her dirt-stained arms. "By the way," she said. "Uncle Will wants to take everyone out for dinner tonight, his treat. Melanie asked if Kevin could come, so he wondered if you wanted to ask anyone special."

Christina groaned. "I don't have anyone special."

"Oh?" Ashleigh's eyebrows went up.

"Dylan's not speaking to me because I wouldn't give him back his bat because he was mad and using it too much on Dakota," Christina said in a rush.

"Slow down," Ashleigh said. "And start from the beginning."

Christina told her everything, from the show Sunday to Dakota refusing the narrow jump on Thursday. Ashleigh leaned against the wall and listened.

"I think Dylan should have lowered the jump or made it into a cross-rail that Dakota could just walk over. I know he was refusing because he was scared," Christina finished.

Ashleigh wrinkled her forehead.

"I'm right, aren't I?" For the first time, Christina felt a little less certain.

"Maybe, but it's hard to judge without knowing more about Dakota. And you've always told me that Dylan is a good horseman."

Christina stopped rinsing Sterling as she tried to organize her thoughts. "He is . . . usually. Only this time I think he was more concerned about how he looked in front of Chad than thinking about what Dakota needed."

"Peer pressure," her mom said, sighing. "It can drive people into doing stupid or dangerous things. Take Melanie, for example."

Her mother was referring to the incident that had sent Melanie to Whitebrook Farm this summer. Her

114

cousin and a friend had snuck horses out of a stable in New York City for a moonlight ride. At the last minute, Melanie hadn't wanted to go through with the plan, but her friend pressured her to keep going, and Melanie's horse ended up being hit by a taxi.

"But Dylan's used to getting grief from Chad. It doesn't explain why he's starting to be a show-off."

"It's hard for you or me to tell what it's like to be a teenage boy in what is mostly a girl's sport. Ask Dad to tell you sometime about the teasing he had to go through."

Christina thought about the games she'd watched this week. Chad, Jacob, and a few of the other guys on the team *did* give Dylan a hard time about having to ride after soccer instead of hanging out with them, but Dylan didn't act like he minded. "Kevin rides, too, but he's okay about it."

Ashleigh pushed away from the wall, automatically brushing off her back. "With Kevin, it's a family business and not so much up for discussion."

That was true. When Kevin said he had to get back to the farm on Wednesday, nobody gave him any grief. "Well, I think it's stupid. Boys have as much right to like horses as girls."

Her mother nodded. "So let Dylan know. It's hard to be different, especially at your age. He needs all the support he can get."

Christina nodded. "But do I have to invite him to dinner?"

"Of course not." Ashleigh grinned. "I'm not ready for all this teenager stuff, anyway."

Christina pressed her cheek against Sterling's damp neck. "I don't know if I'm ready, either," she admitted.

The good thing about going out to eat was that Christina didn't have time to feel nervous about the event the next day. Melanie, Kevin, and Christina pumped Uncle Will for the latest gossip about the famous rock bands he helped produce, and Susan had them in stitches telling about Uncle Will being dragged from the sound booth to sing back-up on a song during a recording session.

"There he was in his three-piece suit shaking and jumping up and down like a rock star," Susan teased.

"But I was great," Uncle Will protested. "They kept the track, didn't they?" When he took Susan's hand and smiled at her, someone kicked Christina under the table. She looked across at Melanie, who grinned and tapped the third finger on her left hand. Christina smiled, too. Something told her she would be going to New York, soon. Maybe Mom would let her buy a long dress for the wedding.

"Did Kevin tell you the Angels lost?" Melanie whispered after they excused themselves to go to the ladies room.

Christina had deliberately stayed away from their last two games because she was upset with Dylan. A guilty wave passed through her, as if she were responsible for messing up their record. "That's too bad. They were so close to making the playoffs."

"They're still going to be in them, though, because two other teams had four wins and one loss, too." Melanie poked her in the ribs. "And you don't have to worry about Dylan missing the event because the game isn't until tomorrow afternoon, after his dressage test."

Maybe everything was going to work out all right after all, Christina thought as she dried her hands. She hoped so, for Dylan's sake.

"Is my hair all tucked in?" Christina asked Katie on Saturday morning. She drew on the white cotton dressage gloves she'd washed in the bathroom sink the night before when they'd gotten back from the restaurant.

Katie ducked behind her and poked at the hair net that kept Christina's doubled-up braid in place. "It's okay."

Katie had already ridden her dressage test and Bree was loaded back onto Mona's four-horse trailer, happily munching hay. Mona was out roaming the grounds with a young horse she'd brought just to look around, not to show. Dylan was brushing Dakota on the other side of the trailer. Neither he or Christina had mentioned Thursday's incident with the bat, but it was standing between them like a wall. Christina noticed that both of them were talking to Katie more than each other.

She inspected Sterling one more time. The mare's dapples gleamed like a pile of silver dollars in the late morning sun. Thirty-two tiny black braids marched down her neck, accenting her newly muscled curve. The well-worn saddle leather was burnished to a chocolaty-brown glow that stood out against the snowy-white dressage pad she saved for shows.

After Katie gave her a leg-up so she wouldn't get her white breeches dirty, Christina scanned the crowd to see if her parents had come yet. She didn't see their car, but that was okay. They'd find her as soon as they got here.

"Have a good ride," someone called as she started across the field to the dressage arena.

Christina looked back and saw Dylan waving with a brush in his hand. "Thanks," she said, adding, "You too," in case she didn't see him before he went in. There were five horses between Sterling's dressage time and Dakota's.

I guess we've made up, Christina thought as she rode toward the dressage arena, glad to put the incident behind them. She leaned forward to give Sterling a pat.

Now that the weight of the fight was off her shoulders, a thrill of excitement ran down her back and she could feel Sterling's eagerness as they walked along under the robin's-egg blue sky. Everything was perfect.

When the judge rang the little bell for Sterling to go into the dressage arena, Christina straightened in the saddle and lifted her chin. "This is it, girl," she said, asking for a bend as they turned at the A marker.

Sterling seemed to understand the importance of the

occasion. She started down the centerline like a pro, halting at X without the usual swish of her tail. Christina saluted the judge and pressed Sterling forward. The mare's hind end wiggled as they approached the C end of the arena. Sterling was still suspicious of the scribe in the broad-brimmed hat who was writing down the judge's comments, even though Christina had given her a few seconds to look in the judge's box before they started the test.

You pay attention to me, Christina silently told Sterling, communicating with her hands and legs. Sterling listened, lifting her back and settling into a workmanlike trot. As long as Christina kept riding half-halts, she was able to keep the mare's attention on the test instead of the horses and the spectators. And when they did their changes of rein down the diagonal—Sterling's back round and relaxed, her neck bent at the poll as she softly mouthed the bit—Christina didn't need to pretend a puppeteer was pulling her tall in the saddle. She felt like a Grand Prix rider: tall, elegant, and in perfect harmony with her horse.

"That was terrific, honey," Ashleigh exclaimed, meeting her as they left the arena.

Christina's jaw hurt from grinning so much. "It was even better than her test at camp, wasn't it, Mike? Did you get it on tape?" Ashleigh went on.

Her father nodded, holding up the small camcorder.

"Thanks for coming to watch me ride," Christina said to Uncle Will and Susan, who had gotten up early to come with her parents. Christina had only waved to them before the test because they drove in while she was warming up.

"We wouldn't have missed it for the world," Susan said, smiling from a safe distance away. "You look so professional in your outfit."

Uncle Will tousled Melanie's hair. "You wouldn't have even recognized this munchkin when she was all decked out in her riding clothes at the camp show."

"Da-ad," Melanie complained, but she was grinning when she turned to Christina. "Want some help putting Sterling away?"

Christina looked at Melanie's sandals. "No, thanks. She might step on you."

Her cousin leaned against Uncle Will. "Better hurry, then. Dylan's already warming up."

Christina rode back to the trailer, quickly untacking Sterling and sponging the sweat off her back. "You're a real champion, you know that?" she murmured, taking a second to kiss the pink snip on her muzzle before swapping the bridle with her halter. Sterling rubbed her head against Christina's shirt, always ready to take advantage of her good mood. "That's okay," Christina said, looking at the foamy mark the mare had left on her white shirt. "You're entitled."

Sterling wasn't cool enough to load onto the trailer, so Christina jogged her back to the dressage area. She wished she'd had time to switch from her tall riding boots to her sneakers.

The horse before Dylan was just finishing his test when Christina and Sterling came up. Dylan was standing outside the roped area that separated the dressage ring from the spectators.

He seemed different in his dressage clothes. More grown-up than when he was wearing a T-shirt and shorts or breeches. His shoulders looked broad in the neatly tailored black hunt-coat. The white shirt and dark tie accented his Adam's apple. When he saw Christina, his serious look disappeared with a big smile.

"You had a nice test," he said. "I watched it from the warm-up area."

"Thanks." Christina dropped her eyes to Dakota. "How's he going today?"

"Good," Dylan said, reaching out with a gloved white hand to stroke his neck. "Real good." He gathered his reins and Dakota's head came up, alert and ready as he watched the last horse leave the arena. "Gotta go," Dylan said, squeezing him forward.

"Smile. Your mom's taping you." Christina waved at Dylan's mother.

Dylan nodded as he asked Dakota for a trot. Christina watched his fluid motion as he rose and fell to Dakota's strides.

If Sterling's test was good, Dakota's was brilliant. The big Quarter Horse moved like he had a metronome in his head, his hind legs reaching well under his body as he went from walk to trot to canter with hardly a toss of his head. When Dylan halted at G and saluted at the end of the test, Christina let out a cheer that sent Sterling's head up with a mouthful of grass to see what all the commotion was.

Christina stayed on the sidelines while Dylan's parents fussed over him. "I'd better get this guy back," Dylan said finally, catching Christina's eye and smiling.

His father looked at his watch. "Think you'll be ready to leave in a half hour? That will give us enough time to grab some lunch before the game."

Christina moved Sterling closer. "Aren't you going to walk the cross-country course with us?" Even though the horses couldn't see the jumps before they had to go over them tomorrow, the riders could. Mona said she'd meet them when Dylan's test was through so she could give them pointers as they walked the course.

"I guess I should," Dylan said, turning to his parents. "Could we just grab something to eat on the way?"

"As long as you're ready to leave in an hour," Mr. Becker said. "You don't want to hold up your team."

"So, did he look good?" Dylan was the first to break the silence as they walked back to the trailer with the horses.

"Yeah," Christina said. "If you ever decide you don't want to jump anymore, he'd make a good dressage horse."

"He's a real ham." Dylan's eyes crinkled when he smiled. "He likes dressage best when there's an audience. Everything about him feels bigger when he starts up the centerline."

"Do you think he's ready for the jumping tomorrow?" Christina said, thinking about the narrow jump.

"I think so." Dylan patted Dakota's neck. "I lowered it like you said and made him walk and trot over it a few times."

"Good. I'm glad it worked."

Dylan looked sideways at her. "I know I shouldn't have taken out my anger on Dakota the other day. I hate it when I lose my temper."

"Me too," Christina said, glad that the bat thing was out in the open now. "I mean, I don't like it when I lose my temper, either."

"Yeah, well." Dylan faltered a little. "I'm not going to do it again. Ever." He draped his arm over Dakota's neck as they walked along. "At least I'm going to try not to. You coming to the game today?"

"I want to," Christina said, "but by the time we finish here and get the horses back, it will probably be too late."

"If you come with Katie and her mother, you might catch the second half at least."

Christina was tempted, even though she knew it meant rushing to get her tack cleaned and stuff ready for tomorrow's cross-country and show jumping phases. "I'll try."

"Good." Dylan paused. "It's more fun when you're there." He reached for Christina's hand and squeezed.

When the horses were cooled off, loaded onto the trailer, and fed some hay, Christina, Katie, and Dylan changed out of their tall leather boots into sneakers and walked down the road to the cross-country field to meet Mona. As soon as they got to the starting box—an eight-foot square enclosed by three sections of fence with the fourth side left open—Mona began.

"Don't take your horses into the box until the starter gives you the thirty-second warning. Then walk in and face the back. Take your time turning and leave the box at a trot." She looked at Christina as she paused to take a breath. "You may want to walk Sterling out of the box. The last thing you want to do is gun her like she's in a race."

Christina nodded. At camp, she'd showed off a little, letting Sterling explode out of the box. It had taken her two fences to get her mare under control again.

"The first time you walk a course, you'll be studying each fence and planning how you're going to approach it," Mona continued as they neared the first jump. It was a long brush-jump with each of the three sections a step taller than the one on the left. The long-needled pine branches were stuffed into a frame made of saplings lashed together with rope. The lowest part was flagged for novice since it had a white background with a black number.

"This looks easy enough," Dylan said, kicking a rock away from the take-off area.

"Technically, yes," Mona agreed. "But because Dakota might be paying more attention to the horses he's leaving behind than the jump, you'll need to ride to the fence firmly and look out for trouble. Katie, what line are you going to use coming into this jump?"

"I don't know. A straight one, I guess."

"Better to think of a slight angle, aiming more toward the middle of the brush instead of the end you'll be jumping. She'll be less likely to duck out on the side that way."

Christina didn't worry too much about Sterling trying to run out. Running away with her was a more likely risk.

"And, Christina," Mona said as if she were reading her mind. "Your greatest challenge is going to be keeping from getting into a tug-of-war with Sterling around the course. You'll need to rely on your seat and back more than your hands to rebalance Sterling before each fence."

By the time they'd gotten to the tenth jump, Dylan was looking at his watch. "I've got to meet my parents in ten minutes."

Mona shook her head. "You'll need to get Christina or Katie to fill you in on the last four jumps, then. I'll be tied up fence-judging in the morning."

"I can look at them now as I jog back," Dylan said.

"You should leave yourself enough time to walk the course again at least two times before you ride it tomorrow morning," Mona warned. "The better prepared you are, the better chance you'll have of getting your horses around safely," she said, including Christina and Katie in her look. "These jumps look spread apart now, when we're walking. You won't have as much time to think when you're in a hand gallop."

"Okay, thanks." Dylan was already walking away. He turned and disappeared down the sandy trail.

Mona frowned. "Riding is certainly taking a back seat in his life these days."

"He's discovered dirt bikes," Katie said. "I heard he's trying out another one after the game today."

"Hmm," Mona said. She shrugged, then walked on. "For the sawmill fence, you'll want to aim for that oak tree so they're coming up the hill at it."

Christina had a hard time concentrating on what Mona was saying. One minute, Dylan was all psyched about riding, and the next minute it seemed like he cared more about soccer or dirt bikes than Dakota. She hoped that when the all-star games were over, Dylan would start acting like himself again.

CHRISTINA CALLED HER MOTHER AS SOON AS THEY GOT back from the event and unloaded the horses. Sterling was spending Saturday night at Gardener Farm to save Mona from having to pick her up in the morning.

"Hello, Mom?" Christina said. "May I go with the Garritys to watch the last half of the soccer game? Mrs. Garrity followed us back from the show." Katie jigged beside her.

"I'd rather you didn't, honey," Ashleigh said. "I know you have things to do to get ready for tomorrow, and I don't want you to put them off until after dinner. It would be a shame to rush yourself and end up forgetting something for your big day, don't you think?"

"I guess you're right," Christina said, shaking her head at Katie. Katie made a long face, then waved good-bye as she ran to her mother's car.

By the time they drive to Bradford for the game, it will be half over, anyway, Christina told herself after she'd hung up the phone. Might as well clean her tack.

It was peaceful in the barn with only an occasional stamping hoof or swishing tail. Christina liked having the place to herself. As she worked the saddle-soap into the buttery smooth leather, she wondered how the game was going.

An hour and a half later when Christina had finished her tack and was saying good-bye to Sterling, two car doors slammed. She was standing at the stall door as Katie and Dylan ran into the barn.

"They won," Katie shrieked. "You should have seen it, Chris. Chad made the winning goal a second before the airhorn went off."

Dylan was pumped up, too. "We're tied for first. If we win the play-off game, we'll be the best soccer team in the whole county," he said.

"Shoot," Christina said. "I wish I could have watched you guys play. Did Katie tell you that my Mom wouldn't let me come?"

"Yeah." Dylan looked sad for about two seconds before he grinned again. "The final game is tomorrow, so maybe you can watch that." He peeked into Dakota's stall. "Hey, thanks for undoing his braids."

"Tomorrow!" Christina said. "What about the event?"

"The game's not until two-thirty. My cross-country time is ten twenty-four, and the stadium jumping is supposed to be right after."

"But we don't have assigned times for stadium. What if they take a long lunch break or something?"

Dylan scratched Dakota behind the ears, and the chestnut flipped up his top lip in bliss. "They won't," Dylan said.

"I hope not," Christina said, turning to Katie. "Did you tell Dylan where he stands after dressage?"

Her friend clasped a hand over her mouth. "I totally forgot. They were playing when I got there, and afterward we were so excited about winning."

"Good or bad?" Dylan said.

"Good." Christina dug the dressage test with the judge's comments and score out of her pocket. "Dakota's second, so far."

"Who-ee," Dylan said, punching the air. "Out of how many?"

"Twenty-four." Christina watched as Dylan read through the comments.

"And in case you're interested, Bree is eighth and Sterling is twelfth," Katie teased.

"Twelfth?" Dylan looked surprised. "Sterling had a nice test. I thought she'd place higher than that."

"Me too," Christina admitted. "But the judge said she was tense through her back."

"That's too bad," Dylan said.

"But the event's only a third over," Christina reminded him. "And the harder parts are left. If you get any penalties over cross-country or stadium, you might slip back out of the ribbons."

"I can handle it, as long as you'll take care of Dakota for me again after I'm done so I can get to the warm-up before the game. I'll owe you one."

Christina let out a gigantic sigh. "You mean, you'll owe me two."

It must have rained all night, Christina thought, dodging puddles in the road as she walked to Gardener Farm early Sunday morning. Yesterday's gray clouds had been replaced by frothy white ones that the wind whipped through the sky. With any luck, the ground would be dry before ten o'clock when she was scheduled to ride cross-country.

"Morning," Christina said as she stepped into Mona's barn. She was the first one there, except for Matt, who had already grained and hayed the horses and was picking out the stalls.

"Better grab a sponge and bucket," Matt said, pushing his baseball cap back as he scratched between his eyebrows with the back of his hand. "Sterling found a dirty spot to lie down on."

"Ster-ling," Christina complained when she saw the brown stain on the mare's hindquarters. "Couldn't you have stayed clean for one more night?" She broke a carrot in thirds, enjoying the velvety-soft tickle of Sterling's lips as she swept the treat away.

By the time Sterling had been returned to her former pewter sheen, Katie was dropped off.

"I think I'm going to throw up," she said, dropping her gym bag in the middle of the aisle. "I don't think I'm cut out to go cross-country."

"You'll be fine," Christina assured her. "Remember how much smaller the jumps looked when we walked the course the third time yesterday?"

"Still, I wish I wasn't going before you." Katie sighed. "Do you think they'd notice if I hid after the second jump and waited until I could follow you and Sterling over the rest?"

Christina laughed. "With a judge and walkie-talkie at every jump and a timer at the starting gate and finish flags, you *might* be missed."

Dylan came whistling into the barn next. "How's my man?" he said as he rubbed Dakota's face. "Ready to whip butt?"

"Pretty big talk from someone who only walked the cross-country course once," Christina teased as she led Sterling out to the aisle to put on her padded shipping-boots.

"I thought you were the one who is so big on positive thinking," Dylan said. He was already dressed for cross-country with a green and white rugby jersey tucked into his fawn-colored breeches. His tall black boots weren't polished, but it wouldn't count against him. Riders were allowed to be more casual for the cross-country phase of the event.

Still, Christina was taking care with her turn-out. She had slipped a pair of painter's pants over her breeches to keep them clean, and her freshly buffed boots were safely tucked into her backpack until it was time to ride. When they got to the show, she would duck into the trailer to change from her barn T-shirt into the red and white polo shirt that matched her striped hat cover and Sterling's galloping boots.

"There's a difference between positive thinking and wishful thinking," Christina retorted. "Don't hurt my horse," she said, ducking behind Sterling when Dylan jokingly threatened her with a dandy brush.

When they were ready to go, Sterling practically leaped onto the trailer, with Dakota and Seabreeze going up behind sedately.

"I see *somebody*'s eager to jump," Mona commented dryly as they fastened the horses, securing the partitions between them. As soon as the ramp was up and the saddles and bridles were counted, Christina and Dylan piled into the back of the truck's extended cab. Katie sat in front since her stomach was still feeling queasy.

"Buckle up," Mona reminded them as she started the engine and crept down the driveway. She was a big believer in starting out slowly so the horses could find their balance. But soon they were on the highway, Christina's stomach fluttering with excitement over the day ahead.

"Now I don't want anybody wiping out in the mud and getting the inside of this truck dirty on the way home," Mona said as she rummaged through the hamburger wrappers and empty soda cans on the floor for her sunglasses. She didn't mean it about the truck, of course. Mona wasn't known for her housekeeping—or truck-keeping in this case. It was a standard joke around Gardener Farm that the barn was the cleanest place to eat.

"Seriously, though, you need to ride carefully after all the rain last night. I'm not worried about the jumps themselves, because most of them have sand and gravel on the take-off and landing sides, but the ground in between might be slick in spots." She glanced at Christina and Dylan in the rearview mirror. "You have plenty of time to get around the course without time faults at the novice level, so don't ride too fast. If the ground looks soft anywhere, it would be better to trot or walk than risk pulling a tendon in your horses' legs."

When they got to the show, Mona helped them unpack their stuff before grabbing her folding chair and backpack and heading off for a long morning of jump judging. Because cross-country was spread out over several miles, there had to be a person at each jump, watching to make certain the horses cleared the fence. Christina had helped jump judge once, and she knew it got monotonous sitting in the grass fifteen feet away from a jump, checking off each horse on the clipboard as they galloped away after jumping the fence. Of course, sometimes the horses would refuse or fall, or a rider would get hurt and the judge would have to radio for the ambulance or catch the horse. The day she had helped, a woman had broken her leg and

Christina led her horse back to the barn while the rider was taken to the hospital. She hoped there wouldn't be any accidents today.

"And have fun," Mona said as she raced for the Porta Potti before hiking to her jump.

"Now she tells us," Katie said with a weak smile.

"Go ahead and unload Bree." Christina gave her a friendly push. "You'll feel better when you're doing something." She looked at her watch and saw that she had an hour before she had to start tacking up Sterling. Should she walk the cross-country one more time? Maybe she could get Dylan to walk it with her.

"Could you hold Bree for a second?" Katie said, practically throwing the lead rope at Christina. "I have to go to the bathroom."

Maybe she'd better stay and help Katie get ready instead. Her friend needed all the moral support she could get. "Hey, Dylan."

"What?" he said, peering from behind the trailer with a pitchfork in his hand. He was picking out the manure from the back of the trailer to cut down on the flies.

"Do you want to walk the course again? You've got time."

Dylan was thinking about it when a car pulled up next to the trailer. Chad climbed out of the passenger side.

"Jeez, Becker. You have to do the grunt work, too?" Chad waved a hand in front of his nose like he could smell the manure from where he was standing.

"You come to groom for me, Walker?" Dylan said, holding out the pitchfork.

Chad had a pained look on his face. "No thanks. I'm here to make sure you get to the game on time."

Dylan laughed. "You're a few hours early, don't you think?"

"Well, you know. I thought I might check out the sights, too." He stooped over so he could lean into the car. "Thanks for the ride, Dad."

Mr. Walker opened the driver's side door and stuck his head out. "Now I don't want to hear that my star goalie has been stepped on by a horse," he called to Dylan.

"No, sir," Dylan said. "I won't mess up."

"Okay, then. I'll be back at one." He nodded to Christina, then got back in the car and left.

One o'clock. That was cutting it close, Christina thought, bending to undo the Velcro on Bree's shipping boot.

When Katie saw Chad, she perked up and lost that greenish, scared look. She put him to work right away, fetching her saddle and things and holding Bree while she tacked up.

"I've been replaced," Christina said.

Katie looked worried. "You don't mind, do you?"

"No," she said, laughing. "I'll see you when you get to the starting box."

She climbed up into the trailer through the side

escape door to check Sterling before she left, but the mare hardly gave her the time of day. She was more interested in hanging her head out the other door, whinnying to horses as she looked around.

Chad, Katie, and Dylan were having a play-by-play rehash of yesterday's soccer win. "I'm going to walk up and watch some of the cross-country," Christina said to Dylan when she could get a word in edgewise. "Want to come?"

"Naw," Dylan said, sticking out his boot. "I didn't bring sneakers."

Christina knew what he meant—riding boots were designed to be comfortable for riding, not walking—but she thought it was a pretty lame excuse for not going over the course again. "Okay, then. I'll see you."

When she got to the field where the cross-country started, she decided to hang around the announcer's box instead of walking the course again. It was fun to see the horses jump the first fence, then follow their progress through the incoming reports: "Horse twenty-one is clean over the stone wall. Horse twenty-one almost had a run out at the sawmill, but he made it over, no faults."

"How's the footing?" she asked a rider who was leading a mud-splashed horse.

"Not too bad. It was a little messy after the cordwood fence and there are big puddles in the field along the river, but all in all, it was fine. Of course, he's got studs in his shoes," the woman said over her shoulder as they walked away.

Studs were small, metal pieces that were screwed into the bottom of horses' shoes to give them better traction. Racehorses used them a lot on muddy tracks. Sterling, Bree, and Dakota just had regular shoes, though.

By the time Katie rode up, Christina had a pretty good idea of where the trouble spots might be. She told Katie about them after Bree was warmed up.

"Watch that last turn over there, too. It looks okay, but I've seen a couple of horses skid in the grass."

"Smile, honey," Katie's mother said, holding up a camera. Christina hadn't even noticed Katie's parents arrive. Chad and Dylan were there, too.

"Horse number eighty-two. You're on deck," the timer said. That meant that Katie was going after the horse that was just entering the box.

"Oh my gosh," Katie said. "I'm so nervous."

"Want me to hop up behind you and keep you company?" Chad offered.

Katie made a face. "Yeah, that would be a big help." But his joke had done the trick and Katie was smiling when she went into the box. And when the timer said, *Go,* Katie and Seabreeze headed toward the first fence and sailed over it without a snag.

"Yay, Katie!" Christina yelled as they galloped away.

"Man, I don't think I could do that," Chad said in a rare moment of humility.

They could only see the first and last jumps from the starting area, but they followed Katie's progress over the radios. By the time they were waiting for her to appear at the top of the last hill, it sounded like Katie and Bree had gotten over all the fences so far.

"There she is," Dylan said as Katie's green and purple hat cover came into view. Bree galloped over the crest of the hill, then dropped back to a trot as they made their way down the tractor road to the field where the last fence awaited them. Bree's strides were short, like she was taking extra care not to slip.

When they reached the bottom and made a ninety-degree turn to the right, Christina wondered if Bree was bobbing her head a little the way horses do when they put their weight on a leg that is bothering them. But then Katie pushed her into a canter and Christina didn't see the bobbing anymore. They took the fruit stand—really a long box with bins of apples, bananas, and oranges painted on—without faltering and cantered on through the finish flags.

"We made it," Katie shouted across the field as she flung herself off. Christina, Dylan, and Chad ran up to congratulate her as she was loosening the girth on her saddle.

"How was it?" Christina said.

"Great!" Katie flipped the reins over Bree's head and started walking her to cool off. The mare was blowing hard after her run, and her already dark coat was black with sweat. "She jumped everything."

Katie's parents came up as they walked along the

pasture to the road. When Christina dropped back, she noticed Bree's head bobbing again.

"Katie. Hold up," Christina called. "I think she's a little off."

Katie stopped and looked back at Bree. "Shoot. She pulled a shoe," Katie said, picking up Bree's left front foot to inspect the damage. "I bet that's what happened when she stumbled in the mud before the Helsinki fence. She must have stepped on the shoe from behind and flipped it off."

"Is this a problem, honey?" her mother said.

"It means I can't finish the event." Katie looked like she was going to cry as she patted Bree's neck.

"I saw a farrier set up by the barn. He could probably tack the shoe back on," Dylan said.

"If we can find it." Katie didn't sound hopeful.

"Tell me where to look, and I'll go get it," Chad offered.

"I'd help, but I have to get Sterling ready." Christina felt bad to be running out on Katie.

But Katie smiled. "Chad can get it. You'd better get back to the trailer."

"I might as well come, too," Dylan said, following Christina to the road. "Dakota won't like it when Sterling leaves and he's by himself."

"I wish I could have talked to Katie more about the course," Christina said as they moved out onto the pavement so a horse and rider could go by on the sandy shoulder.

"Don't worry so much," Dylan said.

"I'm not."

"Then why are you making such a big deal about cross-country?"

Christina could see Sterling watching her from the trailer. "Because it *is* a big deal. At least it is to me."

"What do you mean by that?"

Christina turned and looked Dylan right in the eyes. "I mean, eventing is important to me."

"It's important to me, too."

"But not important enough to walk the course so you have a better chance of getting Dakota around safely?"

"I can't help it if the play-offs were scheduled for this weekend, can I?"

Christina could see the muscles in his jaw tense.

"It's not just that," she said, starting to walk again. "It's just that you don't seem very excited about riding any more."

"Well, I am." Dylan's voice was defensive. "I've just been busy, that's all. Horses aren't my whole life, you know."

"I know." Christina sighed.

10

CHRISTINA FELT BETTER ONCE SHE GOT ON STERLING AND headed to the cross-country field, even though the mare was wound up tighter than a rubber band. Sterling walked and jigged most of the way down the road, and by the time Christina turned into the gate of the warm-up area, she was tired of fighting. Mona might disapprove, but Christina decided to let Sterling canter her warm-up for cross-country.

"Okay, girl. But you've got to go easy," Christina said, planting her hands halfway up Sterling's neck and letting her elbows open and close with the movement of Sterling's canter. When the mare realized Christina wasn't going to pull her back, she relaxed a little, settling into a rhythmic tempo as she blew out through her nose with each stride. Christina kept her along the edge of the fence, as far away from the other horses that were warming up as possible. She didn't want to give Sterling any opportunities to buck.

When the practice jumps weren't too crowded, Christina cantered Sterling over them a few times, stopping only when she realized that instead of settling down, each jump was getting the mare more excited. "You're warmed up enough," Christina declared as she managed to bring her back to a walk. Sterling raised her head, her ears pricked forward eagerly as she watched a horse leave the starting box.

"Chris!"

Christina turned and saw her mother jogging toward her.

"I got behind a hay truck and didn't think I'd make it on time," Ashleigh said. She patted Sterling's lathered neck. "How's she doing?"

"She's a little crazy, but I think she'll be better once we get started."

"Ninety-eight. You're on deck," a man with a red beard and a clipboard said.

"Thanks," Christina said.

Ashleigh had to stand on tiptoe to give Christina a quick hug. "You be careful now." Her mouth was smiling but her eyes were serious.

"I will," Christina said, tugging the back of her safety vest and pulling it down so it covered her whole spine. Most event people wore the padded vests because the half-inch, dense foam could help distribute the impact of a fall or a horse stepping on them. It was kind of a nuisance to wear but, in an accident, it could mean the difference between walking away with a bruise or being carted off in an ambulance with broken ribs—or worse.

"Thirty seconds."

"Okay, girl," Christina said, smoothing a few errant strands of Sterling's silver-streaked mane. "Let's go." Katie's butterflies must have flown into Christina's stomach, but they were excited rather than scared. Cross-country was the heart of eventing—this was the moment she'd been working toward.

As they walked in a circle around the outside of the starting box, Christina felt on edge, as if she were waiting for the music to stop in musical chairs. When the man with the stopwatch began the ten-second countdown, she brought Sterling into the box and halted, facing the rear.

"Seven . . . six . . . five . . ."

Christina could feel Sterling's heart beating under the saddle. She ran a tongue over her dry lips. *Water would sure taste good right now,* she thought, turning Sterling around so they were facing the first fence.

"Two . . . one," the starter finished. Sterling bunched up her muscles and burst out of the box. They were off.

"Easy, easy," Christina said, riding half-halts with each stride as Sterling stretched across the field. But Sterling wasn't listening. She blasted over the first fence like it was a steeplechase, stumbling as they landed on the other side.

Christina clamped her legs as the mare faltered, then righted herself and surged on. "Whoa, whoa," she said, pulling back on the reins, but Sterling wasn't buying it. It was as if she thought Christina was asking her to go faster, and the mare stretched out and galloped even flatter.

This is bad, Christina thought as the sound of Sterling's thundering hooves flooded her ears. If Sterling tripped or shied going this fast, it would be all over for Christina. She raised her right hand in a pulley rein, finally managing to bring Sterling's head up enough so they could circle.

Sterling shook her head and tried to stretch her neck downward to take control. But Christina kept closing her legs and squeezing with her fingers, asking Sterling to soften her mouth and lift her back. She tried to pretend they were in a dressage ring for a riding test, and sat up taller in the saddle.

Slowly, Sterling began to respond. Her head came up as her canter got rounder and she began to blow through her nose with each stride. When Christina opened her fingers a little, making sure that her body remained back and still, Sterling relaxed and mouthed the bit, waiting for her next command.

"Okay, girl," Christina said, allowing her to go straight again. "Let's do this together."

Sterling lengthened her stride as if she was going to speed up, and Christina forced herself to keep her hands still on the mare's neck. She settled back a bit, reminding Sterling with her seat that she could gallop as long as she did it Christina's way, with her chest up and with most of her weight shifted to her hind legs for balance.

And Sterling listened, falling into the steady, ground-covering stride they had been working on for weeks. They approached the hay wagon—a long bed of hay bales with old-fashioned wagon wheels affixed to each end and a two-by-four handle trailing off on one side—and sailed over it in perfect form.

"Good girl," Christina said, leaning forward to stroke Sterling's neck. Sterling's muscles bunched underneath her as they turned the corner without faltering, her ears pricked as she eagerly carried Christina over a white coop.

It was everything Christina dreamed of, galloping through fields, up and down hills, and jumping one massive fence after another. Her job was to navigate the course, slowing Sterling where a turn could prove to be slippery or helping her rebalance herself after a long gallop between fences. And Sterling's job was to use her own agility and grace to carry them both over the fences safely. Even though the jumps were new to Sterling, the mare followed Christina's commands like the two were of one mind. It was as though Sterling had placed all of her trust into Christina's hands.

By the time they jumped the ditch and started down the long, sandy track that led to the last four jumps, Christina was getting tired. Holding twelve hundred pounds of horse together was a lot of work, and her arms and legs were beginning to tremble with the effort. But Sterling wasn't fading one bit. The mare eagerly looked for the next jump, barely startling when they rounded a bend and surprised some spectators who were walking the course. A man and two kids scattered, jumping off to the side to let Sterling pass by. Christina heard one of them say, "Wow. I want a horse like that someday."

She raised her chin, adrenaline rushing to her limbs as the next fence came into sight. It was the cordwood drop—a solid rectangle of wood stacked four-feet deep. While the jump was less than three feet high where they'd take off, the landing side was more like four-and-a-half-feet down since the ground dropped away immediately after the jump. She needed to prepare Sterling for the downhill jump so they wouldn't take a nosedive.

Mona had advised her to trot into the fence if there was any question of Sterling's balance being too far forward. Christina closed her fingers on the reins and at the same time, she squeezed so Sterling would keep her hind legs well under her as she went into a trot.

But Sterling didn't trot. She lifted her back even more, slowing to a rocking-horse canter and jumping the wood as easily as if it had been on the flat. It felt like forever before Sterling's front feet hit the ground on the other side, and the jar of the landing threw Christina forward onto her neck for a second. Sterling didn't seem to notice. By the time Christina got herself firmly back into the saddle, the water jump was looming in front of her.

"You can do it," Christina said, driving Sterling on with her legs. But the mare needed no urging. She splashed into the dammed-up stream, took two canter strides, and leaped up the bank like she'd never had a problem crossing water earlier in the summer.

"Two more jumps and we're home free," Christina said, the wind whipping her words away. They cantered up the hill, turned sharply left, and flew over the ski jump. This time Christina kept her body back as gravity carried them down the graveled hill. She could see the crowd of horses and people milling around the grassy field below.

"Whoa, whoa, whoa," she said in rhythm with Sterling's strides and the mare put on the brakes. The ground ahead of them was soft and she could see places where the horses before them had dug up the wet turf. Sterling shook her head as if she were puzzled to be pulled up before they got back to the others, but she dropped down to a trot and went around the corner without a problem.

"Okay, girl. Last jump." Christina went back to her half-seat position as Sterling picked up a canter again, the ground flying past as they galloped to the fruit stand. Christina, her eyes trained to the finish flags a hundred feet beyond, didn't notice Sterling drifting to the right of the stand until it was almost too late. That higher part of the jump was flagged for the Training Level division; if Sterling jumped it, they would be eliminated from the event.

Christina clamped her right leg behind the girth, asking Sterling to leg-yield left. The hours in the dressage ring paid off when Christina felt Sterling respond by moving sideways away from her right leg a scant two strides from the fence, and jumping the novice side with inches to spare. When they passed through the finish flags, Christina was so psyched, she could have jumped the whole course again.

"Did you go clean?" Ashleigh called as she ran up.

"Yes," Christina sang out, not even pulling Sterling to a complete halt before she leaped off and loosened the girth a hole so her mare could breathe better. "She's the absolute best!"

"I'm glad you're back safe," Ashleigh said, putting her arm around Christina and pulling her close. "Whew," she said, letting her go again. "Now I understand how your dad feels when I ride a race."

Sterling's nostrils were flared and pink as she puffed beside Christina. The veins stood out under her delicate skin like miniature molehills traveling down her neck and shoulders and onto her legs, but her dark eyes were alert as she walked along.

"You really liked that, didn't you?" Christina said, drinking in the sweet, horsey smell of glycerine mixed with sweat.

Sterling raised her head and whinnied, her muscles

148

warm and taut through Christina's gloved hands. When Dakota answered from the starting area, Dylan turned and waved.

"I didn't see you come in," he said when Christina and Ashleigh got closer. "How'd you do?"

"Clean," Christina said, knowing she was grinning ear to ear like a fool.

Chad took the stem of grass he was chewing out of his mouth. "I found the shoe, but the blacksmith said Bree's got a bruise on the bottom of her foot, so Katie can't finish the event."

"Poor Katie. She must be really bummed."

Dylan nodded. "Yeah. She's back at the trailer with her parents, putting Bree away."

"You're on deck," the guy with the clipboard told Dylan.

"Any last-minute advice?" Dylan said.

"Don't get those sissy pants dirty," Chad teased. "We need you in one piece for the game."

"Watch the grassy places," Christina said. "It's slippery in some spots."

When the timer got down to one, Dylan shouted, "Blast off," and Dakota lurched forward out of the box.

"Ride 'im cowboy," Chad yelled after them as Dakota jumped the first fence and raced across the field.

"I see what you were talking about," Ashleigh said in a quiet voice.

Christina worried as she walked Sterling around,

cooling her off. Dylan was doing just what Mona told them not to do, thinking about speed instead of jumping the fences the right way. Maybe he had slowed down as soon as he was out of their sight. She hoped so, anyway.

The horse just before Dakota had hardly passed through the finish flags and come to a stop before Chad hollered, "Here they come."

Sure enough, Dakota was cantering down the gravel track that led back into the field. Christina watched in alarm as Dylan, making no attempt to check Dakota's speed, burst onto the grass. When Dylan pulled Dakota's head to the right to make the ninety-degree turn, the chestnut's feet slipped out from under him and he fell, skidding sideways across the ground with Dylan's leg pinned under him.

"Oh, no!" Christina yelled. "Here," she said, thrusting Sterling's reins into her mother's hands before turning to run.

Don't let any bones be broken. Don't let any bones be broken, she chanted to herself as she sprinted across the field to where Dakota and Dylan were lying in a heap. Halfway there, as if in answer to her prayer, Dakota's head came up. He threw his front legs out in front of him and jockeyed to a standing position. When she caught hold of his reins, he was shaking himself like a dog, with water flying everywhere. "You okay, bud?" she murmured, scratching his muddy neck.

Dylan was slower getting up. The jump judge squatted beside him, talking, before she helped Dylan to his feet. Everybody over by the starting box cheered when Dylan walked to Dakota.

"Are you all right?" Christina asked as Dylan took Dakota.

"I'm fine. It was a soft landing," he joked, pointing to his mud-streaked side. Dylan looped Dakota's reins back over his head, stuck his foot in the stirrup and remounted. He patted Dakota's neck once and trotted a circle. When Dakota moved out all right, Dylan turned and cantered toward the fence. Christina held her breath as she watched Dakota get in a little too close to the jump before he took off, but they cleared it and cantered over the finish line.

"All right!" Christina said, jogging to catch up. Ashleigh was already there with Sterling, fussing over Dylan with motherly concern.

"Good thing your parents didn't see that," Ashleigh said. "It will be bad enough for them to just hear all about it. I'm going to talk to the technical delegate about posting some sort of warning for that spot."

"I laid my dirt bike down like that once," Chad said as Christina's mother headed off. "Should have seen me trying to dig the dirt out of the handlebars."

"Why did you take that corner so fast?" Christina asked.

Dylan had his back to her as he flipped the stirrup

irons across the saddle so they wouldn't bump Dakota's sides as he walked. "It was a mistake, okay?"

Christina ran her eyes over the chestnut. He was breathing hard from the run and streaked with mud. "Well, I'm glad it didn't cost you your horse."

11

THEY HAD TO WEAR THEIR WHITE SHIRTS AND BLACK HUNT coats for the show-jumping phase of the event. Christina was sticky after walking around the stadium course in the sun. The last thing she wanted to do was put on a hot jacket.

"At least Dylan can ride in Bree's spot," Katie said, looking sad but comfortable in the shorts and tank top she'd brought to change into after the event.

Christina felt bad for her. She'd be devastated if something had happened to keep Sterling from finishing the event. "When we get home, we can look through the Omnibus and see when the next event is," she said, hoping to make Katie feel better.

"I don't know. With school starting, I won't have as much time to get Bree ready."

Christina didn't want to think about having her

time with Sterling crowded by school.

"At least I can get a ride back with Chad and Dylan and watch the whole play-off game," Katie said, cheering up as she walked beside Christina and Sterling to the stadium field.

Christina didn't want to think about soccer, either. "Look. Dylan's about to go in." Something seemed different about Dakota, but she couldn't put her finger on it.

As they came up to the chestnut, Chad was pretending to give Dylan last-minute instructions.

"And try not to lay him down again," Chad said with a straight face. A moment later, he burst out laughing.

"I'll keep him under ninety this time," Dylan joked, avoiding looking at Christina. They hadn't spoken since he finished cross-country an hour and a half before. He trotted into the ring, saluted, then cantered his courtesy circle before facing the first jump.

Dakota seemed like he was holding back, going right up to the base of the fence before making a Herculean effort to get over it without knocking down the rails. Dylan tried to push him on when they landed. Christina could see his legs and seat working to drive him forward, but Dakota hardly responded. By the time they got to the in and out, it was obvious to Christina that Dakota's heart just wasn't in it.

The first obstacle of the in-and-out was a vertical—three yellow-striped poles between two standards.

Dakota jumped it, tried to fit in two canter strides where there should have only been one, and got in too close to the second part—an oxer with a three foot spread. His front legs knocked off the first pole which broke with a splintering sound when he landed on it with his hind feet. He cantered to the next jump—two wishing wells with a bench in between—and slid to a stop.

"Don't hit him," Christina whispered as Dylan turned him away and approached again, his bat still against Dakota's shoulder.

When Dakota refused a second time, Dylan just sat there, even though he was allowed to try one more time before they'd be eliminated. After what seemed like minutes, Dylan finally turned away from the fence. But instead of cantering on, he dismounted, tossed his stirrups over the saddle, and led Dakota out of the ring.

Christina could see a line of red staining the white sock on Dakota's left hind leg. "He's cut," she said, bringing Sterling to the gate.

When Dylan squatted and probed the leg gently with his fingers, Dakota snatched his foot up and tried to move away. Dylan straightened and patted Dakota's neck. "I know it hurts, bud." Then, to Christina, "Do you think he needs stitches?"

"I don't know. I wish my mom was still here," Christina said, remembering how she dealt with similar cuts at Whitebrook when the racehorses clipped each other with the sharp edges of their shoes. But Ashleigh had left after the cross-country to see Uncle Will and Susan off.

"You should probably soak his leg in a bucket of cold water until Mona can check it. If it gets a chance to swell too much, the vet won't be able to stitch it and Dakota will end up with proud flesh." Christina paused. "He seemed really tired out there. I'm glad you didn't try to make him jump."

"Yeah, well . . ." Dylan's voice trailed off and Christina wondered if he was thinking about losing his second-place spot.

Chad ran up. "Come on, Becker. We've got to haul." A car horn honked and Christina looked back. Chad's father was parked by the trailer and Katie was waving at them.

Dylan looked at Christina. "Could you take care of him?"

Christina just stared. How could Dylan bring himself to leave when Dakota was hurt?

"After you ride stadium, I mean. I can stick him on the trailer for now." Dylan's eye twitched.

"You're just going to throw him on the trailer without even washing him off?" Christina looked at the patches of sweat on Dakota's neck and flank.

"Yeah, well, they're waiting for me," Dylan mumbled.

Christina swallowed, but this time the words she was biting back wouldn't go away. "Dakota's waiting, too. Is this is the way you're going to treat him after everything he's done for you—" she broke off as the lump in her throat threatened to dissolve into tears.

"Come on, Chris. What else *can* I do?"

Christina clenched her teeth so hard, she could hear them scrape. "Your soccer team needs you and your horse needs you. You got yourself into this. Now you've got to make a choice."

Dylan stared at his boots for a second before letting his breath out in a long sigh. "I guess you're right."

Before Christina could say anything else, he turned and led Dakota away.

Christina tried to get her mind on the warm-up jumps, but she couldn't stop thinking about Dylan. Was he going to just run out on Dakota, or would he try to explain the situation to Mr. Walker and tell him he'd get to the game as soon as he could? There were five extra players on the team. Couldn't they use a substitute if they had to start the game before Dylan got there?

Mr. Walker's car was gone, but Christina couldn't see Dylan or Dakota around the trailer. Just as she started to ride over to see what Dylan decided, the gate person called Sterling's number.

"Ninety-eight. You're on deck."

How on earth was she going to be able to ride the stadium course when she was worrying about Dakota and Dylan? Fortunately, once Sterling trotted into the arena, Christina got hold of herself and managed to block everything but the jumps out of her mind.

Sterling went like a dream, her ears flicking back and forth as she listened to Christina. But the exhilaration from completing the course with no jumping faults was replaced by emptiness when she took Sterling back to the trailer and saw Dakota standing in the stall next to Bree. His saddle and bridle were off, and it looked like Dylan had thrown a bucket of water over him, but that was it. Dylan had made his choice.

By the time Mona finished jump judging, Christina had finished with Sterling and was entertaining Dakota so he would leave his hurt leg in the bucket of water. She frowned as she examined the cut.

"Why wasn't he wearing galloping boots?"

That's what looked different about him. He hadn't been wearing the protective boots in-stadium. Christina frowned, trying to remember if he'd had them on when Dylan rode him cross-country. "I don't know."

Mona straightened up slowly. "It's borderline deep. I'd better see if there's a vet on the grounds."

Mona returned with a woman in light-green coveralls whom she introduced as Dr. Carter. The vet took a second to visit with Dakota before examining his leg. "It will heal better with some stitches," she said finally.

The vet gave Dakota a shot of tranquilizer. "Not too much, because I want it to wear off before you start home." Christina held Dakota's head while the vet started numbing the leg.

"Nice work, keeping that leg cold," the vet said to Christina after she snipped the thread on the last stitch. "I don't think there'll even be a scar."

"Thanks," Christina said.

It was three-thirty before they were packed up and driving home from the event. "Cheer up," Mona said. "Dakota will live, you and Dylan will be friends again, and everything will turn out fine."

"If you say so." Christina ran her finger over the gold embossed letters on the green satin ribbon.

Mona's eyes flicked off the road for a second. "Sixth out of twenty-four. You must be quite pleased."

"I am," Christina said without a lot of enthusiasm. "Sterling was terrific."

"I was impressed at the way you two looked going over the sawmill. Both of you were so intent on what you were doing, I don't think you even saw me."

Christina smiled, remembering the way Sterling trusted her enough to jump all those strange fences. "She has a lot of heart."

Mona agreed. "That's why I like Thoroughbreds. A good one like Sterling will give you one hundred and twenty percent every time." She felt for her can of soda and took a swig. "I guess it's too late to catch the end of Dylan's game."

The sadness came back, washing away the good feelings she had about Sterling's performance. Christina shrugged. "Probably."

Mona patted Christina's leg. "Why don't you leave

Sterling at my place for the night? I'm sure she'd just as soon not be ridden anymore today, anyway. And if you'll help me unhitch the trailer, I'll give you a ride home."

"Okay," Christina said. Her legs were so tired, she didn't think she could get back on Sterling anyway.

When they got back to Gardener Farm, Christina turned Bree and Sterling out with some hay in a shady paddock so they could roll and move around. She felt sorry for Dakota having to stay in his stall, but Mona wanted to wait a day or two before she let him run around. "Dylan can hand-walk him tomorrow to give him a chance to stretch his legs," Mona said.

Christina lingered next to Sterling after she'd taken the mare's halter off and turned her loose. "Thanks for being so wonderful today," she said, leaning against Sterling's silky shoulder. Sterling sniffed her dirty breeches before rubbing her head up and down Christina's leg. When her itch was satisfied, she raised her nose to Christina's cheek, gently blowing wafts of sweet hay in her face.

Christina leaned forward and kissed Sterling's velvet soft muzzle. She would never get tired of Sterling. Never.

A car door slammed and Christina looked around. Dylan was standing by himself in the driveway. He waved as the car drove off, then turned and saw Christina.

"Where's Dakota?"

"In the barn." She watched him disappear through the door. A few minutes later, Mona came out.

"I think he'd like to talk," she said, pausing by the fence before heading on to the house. "Call me when you're ready to go home."

The barn felt cool and dark after the glare of the late afternoon sun. Christina had long since shed her boots, and her sneakers crept silently down the concrete aisle. She looked in Dakota's stall. "Dylan?"

"Yeah?" He was leaning against the wall on the far side of the hay manger. Dakota was in between them, eating hay.

"So, who won?"

"We did." Dylan didn't sound very happy.

"The vet said there probably won't even be a scar." Dylan mumbled something.

"What?" Christina asked.

"It's my fault." Dylan's voice was muffled.

Christina opened the door and slipped inside the stall.

"I took off his galloping boots after cross-country because there was mud under them, and I forgot to put them back on again. I'm screwing up everything."

"Look. I know I was mad and all, but everyone makes mistakes," she said, sliding down the side of the stall until she was sitting on her heels.

Dylan was silent for so long, Christina started to get up again. "Wait." His voice stopped her.

161

"I still love Dakota, no matter what you think," he said. "But I can't spend my whole life hanging around the barn."

"Nobody expects you to," Christina said.

"I want to, though." Dylan paused, as if he had more to say. "It's different for you."

"What do you mean?"

Dylan sighed. "I mean, nobody thinks twice if a girl wants to hang around horses. Guys are the ones who are expected to do team sports."

"I thought you liked soccer."

"I do. I did. Oh, I don't know." His voice trailed off and he looked down. Christina wondered if he were crying.

She didn't know whether she should approach him or pretend not to notice. After what seemed like forever, she cleared her throat.

"Do you want to be alone?" she asked.

"Yeah."

Christina slipped out of the stall. "Are we still friends?" she whispered, sticking her head back into the stall before leaving.

Dylan didn't answer, but she thought she saw him shake his head.

"Thanks for the ride, Mona," Christina said, closing the truck door. "I'll pick up the rest of my show stuff tomorrow."

"Don't forget Sterling," Mona said with a twinkle in her eye.

"I won't," Christina said, trying to summon a smile. She shouldered her backpack and headed into the house without even looking at the barns. They seemed too empty when Sterling wasn't there.

"I'm home," Christina shouted, opening the screened door off the kitchen. As she dropped her boots on the floor, she could already feel the house's deserted air.

"Hi, honey. How was the event?" Christina said, breaking the empty silence in a pretend conversation with her mother.

"Aside from Bree losing a shoe and going lame, and Dylan not wanting to be friends anymore, it was fine." Christina grabbed a couple of chocolate chip cookies from a jar and tossed her backpack onto the kitchen table. A note fluttered to the floor.

Dad and I had to go look at a filly. We'll grab dinner in Lexington on the way back. Melanie went with the McLeans to the soccer game. They'll stop home to pick you up for the barbecue. Can't wait to hear how your stadium went!

Love, Mom

Christina had forgotten about the barbecue at Chad's. It was the last thing she felt like doing. When

163

Melanie got home, Christina would just tell her she was too tired to go to a party. She could always fry an egg or something for dinner.

When Beth McLean drove up at six, Christina was sitting on the porch swing with a glass of lemonade. Her hair was still wet from the shower and she was wishing she had brought Sterling home from Mona's so there'd be someone to talk to.

"They won," Melanie said, bursting out of the backseat and running up to the porch. Kevin followed. "Four to three. And Kevin had two assists."

"I heard," Christina said. "Congratulations."

"Why aren't you in your bathing suit?" Melanie asked. "We're already late because we stopped at the grocery store for chips and stuff."

Christina put her glass down. "I don't really feel like going."

"Why? And don't say it's because you have to ride." Melanie put on her fiercest face.

"Hey, how'd Sterling do in the event?" Kevin said, coming onto the porch.

"Sixth out of twenty-four."

Kevin whistled. "Not too shabby."

Melanie grabbed Christina's arm, pulling her off the swing. "I'm not going to let you poop out on us," she said. "Come on. Let's go get your stuff."

Christina allowed Melanie to drag her into the house. Maybe she should go to the party. The empty house was getting to her and a hamburger sounded a lot more appealing than anything she could scrounge up to eat. Besides, she wanted to talk to Dylan.

The party was in full-swing by the time they got to Chad's house.

"Hey, Kevin. Get your ugly mug over here. They're taking a picture of us for the paper."

Christina followed Melanie out back. Katie was sitting next to the pool, watching the team argue about whether they should have their picture taken in the water or out.

"Hi," Christina said, pushing Katie's legs over so she could sit at the bottom of the chaise. She scanned the crowd for Dylan.

Katie brushed the bangs away from her eyes and smiled. "Hey, Chris. You should have seen the goal kick Dylan made. He sent it all the way up the field to Chad, who scored the winning goal." Her dimples deepened as she watched Chad line everyone up along the diving board.

"Great," Christina said, spotting Dylan by the grill. He didn't look particularly miserable as he talked to Matt Jarvis, who was now hobbling around with crutches and a splint instead of a cast. When Matt's twin sister, April, joined them, a terrible thought went through Christina's head. Maybe that whole thing in the barn was just Dylan's way of breaking up with her.

"Thanks for taking Bree home for me," Katie said,

with her eyes still focused on Chad. Then she hit herself in the head with the palm of her hand. "Oh my gosh, I forgot to ask how you and Sterling finished."

"Sixth," Christina said. "If you and Bree hadn't had to drop out, I probably wouldn't have finished as high."

Katie poked her with a toe. "Yes, you would. I don't think I could have gotten Bree around stadium without dropping a rail."

Dylan caught Christina's eye and started to head over, but somebody's father grabbed him to talk— probably about the game. Then the hamburgers and hot dogs were ready and Chad's mother put plates in everyone's hands, shooing them to the picnic tables piled high with chips and salads.

"You know, Dylan," Chad's father said as he spooned a heap of potato salad on his plate. "There's a good summer soccer camp in Maryland just for goalies."

"Oh yeah?" Dylan squirted ketchup on his hamburger, then reached for the mustard.

"I'll tell your father about it the next time we have lunch."

Christina's fork dropped off her plate. When she finished wiping it off with her napkin, Dylan was standing in front of her.

"Anyone sitting here?"

Christina shrugged. "You?" She scooted over on the stone wall to make room.

166

"Listen. I'm sorry about this afternoon," Dylan started as Mr. Walker came over, pulling up a chair.

"You've made a lot of progress playing goal," he told Dylan, gesturing with the hot dog in his hand. "Put your mind to it, and I'll bet you'll get into college on a soccer scholarship some day."

Christina poked at the square of Jell-O salad with her plastic fork as Chad and Jacob wandered over, too. Why didn't everyone just go away so Dylan could finish what he was saying?

"Is Dad telling you about the camp in Maryland? That's where I'm going next summer, too," Chad said as if Dylan were already signed up. "The camp is four weeks, so we'll be back in plenty of time for the school's pre-season soccer in August. Man, I bet we'll be the only ninth graders to make varsity."

"I don't think so," Dylan said.

"Yeah, well, maybe we'd have to go JV the first year. We don't want to make the juniors and seniors look bad." Chad took a swig of soda.

"I mean, I'm not going to play soccer next summer."

Christina looked at Dylan in surprise, but his eyes were on Chad.

Chad glanced at his father, then back at Dylan. "What?"

Dylan laughed, but Christina could tell it was forced. "I can't just hang my horse up in the garage when I'm gone. I need to spend more time with him."

Jacob snorted. "Are you kidding? Every time we finished playing, you were running off to ride."

"Man," Chad said, shaking his head. "How can you let a dumb animal get in the way of something important like soccer?"

Christina could see Dylan's hands tense, but when he spoke, his voice was calm. "Dakota's not just a dumb animal, Chad."

"Maybe not, but riding's a girl thing," Jacob said.

Christina opened her mouth to protest, but Dylan spoke first. "Tell that to Mark Todd and David O'Conner. There are hundreds of men who are world-class riders."

Chad's father nodded. "I've watched them on the sports channel. Is that what you're aiming your sights for, Dylan?"

"I don't know." Dylan studied his plate a second before speaking. "I like soccer, but riding is more important to me. I thought I could do both, but I can't. At least, not as well as I want to." He looked at Christina, and smiled. "That's what I wanted to talk to you about. I did a lot of thinking after you left Mona's this afternoon."

Chad interrupted. "Give me a motorcycle with good brakes any day," he said, shaking his head. "But if that's what works for you—hey, go for it."

The next morning, Dylan was waiting for Christina when she was dropped off at Gardener Farm.

"Hi," she said, suddenly feeling shy. They'd never gotten a chance to finish their conversation at the party.

"Can we talk?"

"Sure." She looked around. "Where to?"

Dylan took her hand and led her to the big pile of clean sawdust that sat in a three-sided concrete bunker behind the barn.

"Here?" Christina said, giggling. "We'd better hope Matt doesn't catch us." The groom didn't let the kids who came for lessons play in the sawdust because they spread it out too much.

"He won't see us," Dylan said, climbing up the golden mountain and disappearing on the other side. Christina scrambled up after him.

"This is great," she said, wiggling in as she sat down. "Like a giant beanbag chair." She loved the piney smell of the sun-warmed sawdust.

"I like to come here and think," Dylan said, settling back, too. He paused before adding, "I'm sorry I've been such a jerk."

"You haven't been a jerk."

Dylan raised his eyebrows.

"Well, maybe a little bit of a jerk," Christina agreed. "But everyone is, sometimes."

Dylan sighed. "I shouldn't have been such a hot-shot, thinking I could be a star soccer player and get ready for an event at the same time. I didn't like what I was doing with Dakota—showing off and losing my temper and all—but I couldn't stop."

Christina sighed. "Mom told me that my dad used to get teased about liking horses, too."

"Really?"

"Yeah. I'd never really thought about how hard it was for guys to do certain kinds of sports before. Can you imagine Jacob's face if you told him you wanted to be a ballet dancer?"

Dylan snorted. "I don't even want to think about it."

"It's not fair," Christina continued. "Boys should be able to dance, or ride, or do any sport they like. Just like girls should be able to play football," she added.

"Thanks," Dylan said.

"For what?"

"For getting mad. You helped me realize that riding *is* an important part of my life."

"I did?" Christina said.

"You did." Dylan leaned over and gave her a soft kiss before jumping up and pulling her to her feet.

"Come on. Dakota and I will walk you and Sterling home."

Christina smiled. She couldn't believe how much she had worried about Dylan's decisions lately. Now everything had worked out all right, just as Mona said it would. She should have trusted him in the first place. He loved horses as much as she did, and now he had made his choice. She felt like whooping out loud. Instead she tugged lightly on his hand and broke into a jog. "Let's go," she said. "We've got lots of riding to do."

DALE BLACKWELL GASQUE has ridden and trained horses for most of her life. As a teenager, she showed in equitation and hunter classes before combined-training events caught her interest. After spending time in England and earning her British Horse Society Assistant Instructor degree, she bought her first Thoroughbred off the track and re-schooled her as a dressage and event horse.

Ms. Gasque is an elementary-school librarian who says the best part of her job is finding good books for kids to read. When she's not in school or at her computer writing horse stories, chances are she's eventing Christopher Robin, her latest ex-racehorse, or trail riding with her husband and two children on their Vermont farm in the mountains.

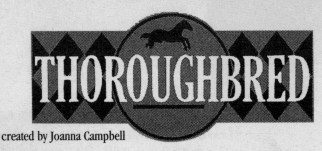

THOROUGHBRED

created by Joanna Campbell

**Read all the books in the Thoroughbred series
and experience the thrill of riding and racing,
along with Ashleigh Griffen, Samantha McLean,
Cindy McLean, and their beloved horses.**

MAIL TO: **HarperCollins Publishers,
P.O. Box 588 Dunmore, PA 18512-0588**

**Visa & MasterCard holders
—call 1-800-331-3761**

Yes, please send me the books I have checked:

❑	**Ashleigh's Hope** 106395-9	.$3.99 U.S./ $4.99 Can.
❑ #1	**A Horse Called Wonder** 106120-4	.$3.99 U.S./ $4.99 Can.
❑ #2	**Wonder's Promise** 106085-2	.$3.99 U.S./ $4.99 Can.
❑ #3	**Wonder's First Race** 106082-8	.$3.99 U.S./ $4.99 Can.
❑ #4	**Wonder's Victory** 106083-6	.$3.99 U.S./ $4.99 Can.
❑ #5	**Ashleigh's Dream** 106737-7	.$3.99 U.S./ $4.99 Can.
❑ #6	**Wonder's Yearling** 106747-4	.$3.99 U.S./ $4.99 Can.
❑ #7	**Samantha's Pride** 106163-8	.$3.99 U.S./ $4.99 Can.
❑ #8	**Sierra's Steeplechase** 106164-6	.$3.99 U.S./ $4.99 Can.
❑ #9	**Pride's Challenge** 106207-3	.$3.99 U.S./ $4.99 Can.
❑ #10	**Pride's Last Race** 106765-2	.$3.99 U.S./ $4.99 Can.
❑ #11	**Wonder's Sister** 106250-2	.$3.99 U.S./ $4.99 Can.
❑ #12	**Shining's Orphan** 106281-2	.$3.99 U.S./ $4.99 Can.
❑ #13	**Cindy's Runaway Colt** 106303-7	.$3.99 U.S./ $4.99 Can.
❑ #14	**Cindy's Glory** 106325-8	.$3.99 U.S./ $4.99 Can.
❑ #15	**Glory's Triumph** 106277-4	.$3.99 U.S./ $4.99 Can.
❑ #16	**Glory in Danger** 106396-7	.$3.99 U.S./ $4.99 Can.
❑ #17	**Ashleigh's Farewell** 106397-5	.$3.99 U.S./ $4.99 Can.
❑ #18	**Glory's Rival** 106398-3	.$3.99 U.S./ $4.99 Can.
❑ #19	**Cindy's Heartbreak** 106489-0	.$3.99 U.S./ $4.99 Can.
❑ #20	**Champion's Spirit** 106490-4	.$3.99 U.S./ $4.99 Can.
❑ #21	**Wonder's Champion** 106491-2	.$3.99 U.S./ $4.99 Can.
❑ #22	**Arabian Challenge** 106492-0	.$3.99 U.S./ $4.99 Can.
❑	**Ashleigh's Christmas Miracle** 106249-9 Super Edition	.$3.99 U.S./ $4.99 Can.
❑	**Ashleigh's Diary** 106292-8 Super Edition	.$3.99 U.S./ $4.99 Can.
❑	**Samantha's Journey** 106494-7 Super Edition	.$4.50 U.S./ $5.50 Can.

Name _____

Address _____

City _____ State _____ Zip _____

SUBTOTAL ....$_____

POSTAGE & HANDLING .$_____

SALES TAX ....$_____
(Add applicable sales tax)

TOTAL ....$_____

Order 4 or more titles and postage & handling is **FREE!** For orders of fewer than 4 books, please
include $2.00 postage & handling. Allow up to 6 weeks for delivery. Remit in U.S. funds.
Do not send cash. Valid in U.S. & Canada. Prices subject to change.   H19311